In Full View

By Scott Duck

Disclaimer

This novel is a work of fiction. The characters, names, incidents, dialogue, and plot are the products of the author's imagination or are used fictitiously. Any resemblance to actual persons or events is purely coincidental.

Dedication

This book is dedicated to my Wife, Lara, and my kids, Nathan, Elizabeth, Jimmy, Chris, and Drake. Lara provided a great deal of assistance in editing the manuscript as well as making several suggestions which helped to make the book better. I would like to thank her for that and for believing in me. I would like to thank my kids for being some of the best kids in the world. God has blessed me with a wonderful family and I thank Him every day for them.

Chapter 1

On the morning of October 1, 2013, Jake Richardson awoke early, while it was still dark. Of course, to him, it was always dark. Jake was blind.

He had a vague impression that he had been awakened by a sound but he wasn't sure.

He rolled over onto his back and his right hand reached out for the iPhone on his night stand. He felt the rubbery sides of the Otter Box case and his index finger moved along the lower portion of the front of the case until he felt the little depression that indicated the home button. He pressed it and, in a clear female voice, the phone said "4:08". As he lay there in the dark, about half a minute later, the phone said "screen locked".

The IPhone had a built in piece of software, called Voice Over. Voice Over was what was known as a screen reader, which allowed a blind person, such as himself, to use the phone just as effectively as someone with perfect eyesight could. The iPhone was just one of the little miracles of technology that made Jake's life much easier and allowed him to do some things that he simply would not otherwise be able to do.

Despite the early hour, Jake decided to go ahead and get the day started. Tomorrow, his brother, Dan, would be taking him to Memphis to have what could turn out to be a miraculous procedure done, the goal of which was to give him his eyesight back. Today though, Jake needed to get some work done.

He sat up on the side of the bed. He stood, turned 90 degrees to the left, walked a few feet, turned left again and walked a few more feet, past the foot of the bed, then turned right and proceeded into the bathroom. He did all of this without touching anything, not even the walls. He did use a cane, when he was out in public, but, here at home, he didn't need it. He did sometimes trail the walls and furniture lightly with his fingers but, with many ambulatory tasks, such as the one that he had just performed, he didn't even need to do that.

When he crossed the threshold of the tiny bathroom, he slowed substantially and proceeded until he felt his waist lightly touch the edge of the counter.

He reached out with his right hand for the place where he knew that his toothbrush lay and he picked it up. He then reached out with his left hand for the place where the tooth paste sat and picked it up. He turned the toothpaste tube up-side-down over the toothbrush and lowered it until he felt the end of the tube touch the brush. He applied the correct amount of pressure as he moved the tube along the bristles of the brush. He placed the brush in his mouth and, sure enough, it had toothpaste on it. Occasionally, when performing this procedure, he ended up with no toothpaste coming out of the tube or the tooth paste ended up going in the sink because everything wasn't lined up quite right. More often than not though, he ended up with the toothpaste where it was intended to go. He brushed his teeth, rinsed, and put everything back where it went, exactly where it had been before, so that he could easily find it next time.

He was only wearing underwear and he stripped that off. Proceeding by feel, he reached into the shower and turned on the water. After the water had time to heat up, he adjusted the temperature to a comfortable level and climbed in. On the shower head hung a caddy, the top portion of which contained a wire enclosure that resembled a shallow basket, which contained his shampoo on the left, shaving cream in the middle, and body wash on the right. A few inches below that was a wire shelf which contained the plastic tray into which his razor snapped. Below the caddy, on the knob that controlled the water, a clean wash cloth was draped.

He shaved first. He reached to the familiar position in the middle of the caddy and picked up the shaving cream with his right hand and squirted a dollop into his left hand. He put the shaving cream back and he lathered his face. He then reached to the bottom of the caddy and picked up the razor with his left hand. With his right hand, he unsnapped the razor from the little plastic tray and he put the tray back in the caddy. He shaved with his right hand, occasionally lightly feeling his face with his left hand in order to check his progress. Once he was satisfied that he had done an adequate job, he again took the little plastic tray with his left hand, snapped the razor back into place with his right hand, put the tray back in the caddy, and rinsed the remaining lather off of his face.

He heard something. Actually, he felt it more than heard it. It was a sort of a dull thudding sound that seemed to reverberate through the frame of the house. He paused and listened but he heard nothing else. Sometimes it sounded and felt like that when someone slammed a door but no one else was in the house. There was a slight chance of thunder storms in the forecast today. Perhaps it had been thunder. It didn't really sound like thunder but he could think of no other explanation.

Continuing to systematically proceed by feel, he lathered and washed his hair and then his body. He then rinsed off and turned the water off.

He pushed the shower curtain aside. He reached out with his left hand and closed his fingers around the soft and slightly furry feeling of the towel that hung on the towel rack, perpendicular to the shower curtain. He dried off and proceeded back into the bedroom, back to the night stand where his iPhone lay.

He picked up the phone and again he pressed the home button. The phone said "4:28". When using an iPhone with the Voice Over screen reader, it was necessary to use different gestures to control the phone than a sighted person would use to control the

3

phone visually. Jake placed his finger at the bottom of the screen, on the slider that is used to unlock the phone. A sighted person would place their finger at the bottom left of the screen and slide to the right to unlock the phone. Jake touched the bottom of the screen. When the phone said "slide to unlock", he did a double tap, which is to say that he touched the screen twice in quick succession, which is the gesture that is used by Voice Over to activate an item, in this case activating the slider in order to unlock the phone.

When he did this, the phone made the unlock sound and said "settings" which was the item that was at the top left of the home screen. Jake flicked right, that is to say that he touched the screen and while keeping his finger on the screen, he moved his finger quickly to the right. This caused Voice Over to move focus to the next item and speak the name of that item, which, in this case, was "contacts, which was the second item on the home screen. He continued to flick right until he got to the color identification app and he double tapped in order to activate it. The phone said "color identifier running".

He turned 180 degrees, walked to the end of the bed, turned left, walked two feet, approximately to the center of the foot of the bed, reached out with his left hand, laid the phone on the bed, turned 90 degrees to the right, now facing the closet door, reached out with his right hand, felt for and grasped the knob, and opened the door.

It was a small closet, about four feet wide by two and a half feet deep, with a shelf at the top and a clothes rod right below that. Jakes clothes were hung on the rod, pants on the left and shirts on the right. He reached out and grabbed a pair of blue jeans. He knew approximately where the jeans were positioned and the denim had a distinct feel. He reached out to the left and hung the jeans on the closet door knob. He decided to wear a polo shirt. It was easy to determine which shirts were polos by feeling of the collars and buttons. He liked polo shirts and had several colors of them.

This is where the phone came in. The app that he had previously activated was a color identification app. With this app running, he could place an object in front of the phone's camera and the phone would tell him the color. He selected a shirt and with his left hand pulled the shirt out a few inches and with his right hand he positioned the phone's camera in front of it. The phone said "red". He repeated the procedure and the phone said "blue". The third time, the phone said "yellow". He stopped there because yellow was his favorite color and he thought that it would be as good a choice as any. He reached out to the left and hung the shirt on the closet door knob, with the pants. He then turned around and put the phone back on the bed.

He proceeded to the dresser, where he extracted underwear, from the bottom middle drawer, and white socks, from the bottom right drawer. If he had wanted black socks, he would have gotten them from the bottom left drawer.

Now that he had selected all of his clothing, he dressed quickly, retrieved the phone from the end of the bed, and went quickly down the hall to the kitchen, lightly trailing the fingers of his right hand along the wall.

Jake usually loved the morning. He loved sipping his coffee, reading the news on his iPhone, and mentally planning the day. This morning, though, he felt a bit unsettled and he wasn't sure why. He supposed that the unidentified sound that he had heard while in the shower had unnerved him. He really did not think that it had been thunder. Still, he could come up with no other explanation. Perhaps he would feel better after his coffee.

The previous night, he had put the coffee in the brew funnel and put the water in the reservoir of the coffee maker. Now, he proceeded to the juncture of the L shaped kitchen counter and advanced his right hand until he was touching the face of the coffee maker. He felt for and pressed the top right button, which was the brew button.

He knew that it would take about ten minutes for the coffee to brew and so he decided to go ahead and start getting things ready in his study for the work day.

Jake was currently an aspiring novelist, as yet unpublished. Writing had not always been his profession. He had a business degree and a little credit toward his MBA. Right out of college, he had been the CFO of a small furniture retailer. He held that job for about five years until, after falling on hard times, the furniture store had been forced to eliminate his position. For a while, he had searched in vain for a similar job. He found that most potential employers did not take seriously a blind person who wanted to do that kind of work, even if they had an impressive track record which demonstrated that they were capable of it. After a while, he resolved to take whatever job that he could find, just anything to pay the bills. He had held various jobs over the years, most recently a job doing medical transcription. That job had recently been eliminated because of budget cuts which had been necessary because of the affordable care act. After that, he had settled on writing as a possible career choice.

Some blind people refused to acknowledge that they had any worth while abilities, relatively content to sit home and draw disability, if they were able to do that. Some others refused to acknowledge that they had any limitations, proclaiming that they could do absolutely anything that a sighted person could do. Jake fell somewhere in the middle of those two extremes.

He knew that he had many abilities that could be valuable to an employer. It was largely a matter of someone giving him a chance to use those abilities. On the other hand, he was realistic concerning the fact that he was relatively limited regarding his possible career choices as compared to someone with normal eyesight. There were

6

many jobs that a blind person simply could not do. He doubted, for instance, that he would ever be able to get a job as a cab driver or a 747 pilot. People do not generally like to be driven or flown around by the braille method, though he thought that some sited people drove by that method. He thought that perhaps he might get a job as the driver of a church bus. What better way to improve the prayer life of the passengers? He didn't really think that was very likely either though, at least not for a while and, in the meantime, while he was waiting on the call from a uniquely enlightened preacher, he thought that he should find something that someone would pay him to do.

He had only recently given serious thought to writing for a living. From his prospective, that would be one of the few professions where he would be on completely equal footing with his sighted peers. He had always been told that he was good at writing. He loved to read, both fiction and nonfiction. When reading a novel, he had occasionally vaguely wondered if he could do that, if he could write a novel, maybe a good one, maybe one that would be right up there with those of his favorite authors (Dean Koontz, Stephen King, John Grisham). Probably not but, hey, one never knew. After losing his most recent job, he decided, what the heck, he would give it a shot.

One of the characters in his novel was blind. One thing that he wanted to accomplish when writing this novel was to accurately portray a blind person. In the real world, sighted people tended to underestimate blind people. In fiction, authors tended to do just the opposite, giving blind characters almost superhuman capabilities. Jake had once read a novel in which one of the characters, who was blind, could hear someone else's heart beat when just standing next to them. Ridiculous. If Jake's sense of hearing was that keen, he could probably get a job working for the CIA as a spy, using his own ears for surveillance equipment. Or maybe he could drive that church bus by sonar, sticking his head out the window and yelling "ping". The truth about most blind people lies between the two extremes of the way that the world perceived them and the way that books portrayed

7

them. Jake thought that, being blind himself, he could give an accurate portrayal, though that was only one goal of the book.

If the procedure that he would be having tomorrow at Vision Biotech turned out to be successful, his blindness would soon be a thing of the past and he would be the first person ever to go from complete blindness to having normal vision, perhaps even better than normal. He could then write a book about the journey from complete darkness into the light. He was quite sure that he could find someone to publish that book. For now though, his current novel in progress called out to him and he had to answer the call.

Jake went into the study. He sat down in front of his laptop computer and opened it. He touched the top left, just above the 1 key. He felt for and pressed the power button.

As he sat and waited for the computer to boot up, he thought that he heard a sound behind him, just for a split second. He swiveled around in his chair. He called out into the darkness "hello". Nothing. He called again. Nothing. He started to get an uneasy feeling. After all, someone could be standing right in front of him and he wouldn't be able to see them. He admonished himself, "Jake, old boy, you have been writing so much that you are starting to act like you are living in your novel".

The computer finished booting up and the operating system made the familiar start-up sound. Jake practically jumped out of his chair. He had to get hold of himself. He swiveled back around to face the computer.

Like his iPhone, his computer ran a piece of screen reader software. The screen reader on the computer was called JAWS, an acronym which stood for "job access with speech". Similarly to the way that he could use Voice Over to access the phone, he could use JAWS to access the computer and perform almost all of the functions that a person with eyesight could.

He checked his E-mail and found nothing of consequence. He then opened the directory which contained his novel in progress. He opened the latest chapter and used the screen reader to read what he had written yesterday. He liked it, though there were a couple of minor changes that he wanted to make. He could now smell the coffee brewing and he decided that he would make the changes after getting his first cup.

As he was about to pass out of the study, he subconsciously raised his left hand and touched the light switch, just to the left of the door. He froze. The switch was in the up position, which meant that the light was on. Being completely blind in both eyes, lacking even light perception, he did not use the lights when no one else was in the house. He tried to remember the last time that someone had been here, in the study, when the lights would have been on. Two or three days previous, his brother, Dan, had been here. They had sat in the study and discussed Jake's upcoming eye procedure. Had the light remained on when Dan had left and been on ever since? Jake didn't know but he was beginning to get the creeps again.

He went down the hall to the kitchen. By feel, he located a cup in the cabinet above the coffee maker and pored himself a cup. He stood there for a second, sipping the coffee, hoping that the hot liquid would help to dispel the chill that was beginning to settle over him. Had that light been on since Dan left? He just didn't know. It was on now. If Dan had not left it on, what did that mean? Should he call Dan and ask if he had turned it off?

He pulled his iPhone out of his pocket and pressed the home button. It announced 4:53. Was Dan up? Probably so, he was an early riser. He unlocked the phone, opened the phone app, and found Dan's name in the list of favorite contacts. He paused before double tapping in order to place the call. Even if Dan was up, which was not a certainty, he probably wouldn't remember whether or not he had turned the light off. People just didn't remember things like that, especially two days later. He locked the phone and put it back in his pocket. Then, he grabbed his coffee and headed back for the study.

As he came into the study, he turned the light off. He sat down again in front of his computer. He decided to read the last page again in order to decide exactly how to make the changes that he wanted to make. As he reached for the keyboard, he felt a small circle of steel pressed against the base of his neck. A voice from behind him and just to his left said "that looks like a pretty good book that you are writing and if you want to live to finish it, do not move".

Chapter 2

One year previous, October 1, 2012.

Dan Richardson sat at his desk at the end of a long day, looking forward to going home. He was one of the founding partners of R and R Accounting. He was very good at what he did and he had made a lot of money doing it. Lately though, he had found it less satisfying.

Dan had grown up in Jackson, Tennessee, a mid-sized town in West Tennessee. He came from a middle class family, the middle of three children of Ramona and Gary Richardson. He had an older brother and a younger sister.

His mother was a house wife and stay at home mom, which was a full time job with overtime. She kept the home fires burning, as the saying goes, while his father spent long hours away from home on business. She was very kind, gentle, and patient. Those were not easy traits to maintain through Dan's teen age years and especially those of his siblings. Dan attributed much of what was good about himself to his mother.

Dan had a lot of respect for his father. He was an attorney, specializing in corporate law. He was a very successful business man, before he retired, but he grew up very poor and never forgot where he came from. Dan had once heard him described as "a tough old geezer but a fair old geezer". Though Dan would not have phrased it in quite that way, he did understand that assessment. To Gary's children, he was stern but kind. Gary tolerated no disobedience or disrespect but he did understand that kids will be kids and, when his kids screwed up, he didn't dwell on it. Gary believed in education and a strong work ethic and he instilled those values in his kids. He expected much from his children but he was willing to do whatever he could to help them to succeed.

Dan's father required him to keep a job while he was in high school and college, although he didn't need the money, in order to teach him the importance of a work ethic. Through some of Gary's business contacts, he was able to get Dan a job working afternoons and Saturdays at Hannon and Associates, a locally owned accounting firm. Dan's friends thought that was strange work for a high school kid. Most of the kids his age who worked were employed at some fast food joint but that just wasn't what Dan wanted to do. He had always been somewhat nerdy and he liked playing with numbers. He wasn't one of those kids who worked ten page algebra problems on the weekends for extra credit. Though he wasn't that nerdy, he liked playing with math in practical application and he was fascinated by business. He sometimes sat in his father's office, with the law firm's financial records and a calculator, playing around with different scenarios, trying to figure out how the firm could make more money. So, working at an accounting firm, even as a part time low level assistant, seemed like a good idea. It turned out to be really good for his bank account. Eight dollars per hour may not have been all that much but his parents were still paying all of his living expenses so he was able to save as much as he wanted. And save he did. By the time he graduated from high school, he had 25 thousand dollars in the bank.

Dan's father believed strongly in education and he encouraged Dan to get as much education as possible. Gary passed his belief in education on pretty effectively and Dan studied as hard as he could, given his work schedule. He knew that he would have to have a pretty good GPA if he wanted a shot at getting into a decent college. He graduated eighth in a high school class of 200, which he thought was not stellar but not too bad.

All that study and work didn't leave Dan with much time for a social life, which didn't really bother him. In high school, he had dated a couple girls but not for long and nothing serious.

Dan attended Union University, a local private university, where he graduated with a bachelor's degree in accounting. He didn't do it the usual way though, at least not the usual way for a kid just out of high school. He did his college course work at night and worked full time at Hannon and Associates during the day. He did this because, by the time that college rolled around, Dan already had pretty grand dreams for himself. He wanted to start his own accounting firm and that would require money. He was used to hard work and he already didn't have a social life. By the end of his undergrad college career, he had added another 100 thousand dollars to his savings.

He decided to continue his education, again taking night classes, now working toward his masters of accountancy. During this time, he continued to work full time at Hannon and Associates. He managed to save up another 50 thousand dollars by the time that he had completed his grad work.

OK, now, here was Dan, a young, talented guy, unattached, with almost 200K in the bank and big plans for his future. West Tennessee had become too small for him, or so he thought at the time. He decided to head for Atlanta. Surprisingly, for all of his careful preparation to this point, he gave no real thought as to why he wanted to go there. He just wanted out of West Tennessee and Atlanta, Georgia sounded like as good a place as any. His mother was convinced that he would be ax murdered within a week, and that was if he was lucky. Her negative sentiment didn't bother him too much, he was used to it. His father said "go give 'em heck tiger". So, with almost 200K in the bank and big dreams in his head, off he went.

Dan had inherited an enterprising spirit from his father and he had always wanted to start his own accounting firm. He went into business with Fred Robinson, a former classmate who had been in his masters program. They started the business with 250 thousand dollars. Dan used 125 thousand dollars of his savings. Fred mortgaged everything that he had and borrowed 125 thousand

13

dollars. They leased a tiny overpriced three room office suite, hired a secretary, and opened R and R accounting.

Startup capital of 250 thousand dollars isn't all that much, not when you have three people to pay and rent to cover in downtown Atlanta, with very few clients.   The first couple years were really rocky and Fred and Dan missed a few pay checks but then things just took off. Within 5 years, R and R Accounting had a net worth of almost a million. Within ten years, there were two more partners and the firm had a worth approaching ten million with 75 CPAs, a support staff of 125, and its own 20 thousand square foot facility in down town Atlanta. Dan was proud of the business that he had helped to build, he loved his work, and he liked most of the people that he worked with. As far as his professional life was concerned, he couldn't have asked for more.

There was a time when this was also true of his personal life. The day that he moved to Atlanta, he stopped at Bob's Burger Barn, about half an hour outside of town, and his life changed forever. Bob's Burger Barn was a sort of old fashion place with a hand full of tables in a small dining area and a counter with stools lined up along it. When he walked in, he took a seat at the counter and studied the menu posted above it for a minute. When the only waitress in the place, who looked as though she had rather be anywhere but there, finally noticed him, he ordered an extra-large one pound cheeseburger, double order of fries, and 40 ounce Coke. He had always had an enormous appetite but, for whatever reason, he could eat pretty much whatever he wanted and still stay right around 200 pounds.

As soon as he had finished ordering, he heard a mousy voice, from his immediate right, say "That's a lot of food!" It was only then that he turned to look at the woman that he had sat beside and he almost fell off of his stool. He thought that she surely had to be the most beautiful thing that he had ever seen in his entire life. She was about 5'5" or 5'6", of slender build, with shoulder length brown hair,

14

blue eyes, and a smile that made the sun look dim. He considered proposing right then and there but he decided that it would be more prudent to settle for talking for a while first. As they talked, among other things, he discovered that her name was Cathy Johnson, she was also from Tennessee, she had also just graduated from college, she was also the middle of three siblings, she had no significant other, and he still thought that marriage might not be a bad idea. He had entered Bob's Burger Barn famished and he left most of his food untouched on the counter but he also left with a promise that Cathy would see him the next night. Six months later, he proposed and six months after that, they were married.

For the first couple years, while R and R Accounting was just getting started, Dan's income wasn't all that great and so Cathy worked to help support them. She had an English degree and she taught English at a local high school. They didn't have all that much but they were happy. When R and R Accounting really took off, Dan made more than enough for them to live on so, with Dan's encouragement, Cathy quit her job.

At the time, the plan was for them to start a family and for Cathy to be a stay at home mom. At first the plan to get the baby on the way was quite simple; Cathy quit taking her birth control pills. They figured that, in just a little while, that would do it. When, after about a year, that didn't do it, Cathy started doing fertility research. They started paying attention to what they ate and they started coordinating their sexual escapades with her monthly cycle. They tried all kinds of things that Cathy came up with in her research and they even came up with a few of their own tricks along the way but, even after two more years, no baby.

Finally, exasperated, they went to see a fertility specialist. They both got poked and prodded in places where they didn't know that they had places. When the test results came back, they were told that nothing was wrong with either of them. They had the tests done again and, again, they were told that nothing was wrong with either of them. They tried for another year and still no baby so they went to a different doctor and repeated everything with the same result. They continued to hope for a while but, after a while, it became clear that, for whatever reason, no baby was forthcoming.

As the years went by, Dan and Cathy began to drift apart. Really, Dan thought that Cathy began to drift away from him. He did his best to prevent it. He was as attentive as he knew how to be. He sent flowers and candy even when there was no occasion. He dropped in just to take her out to lunch. He surprised her with little weekend trips to places that he knew she liked. Still, she became more and more distant.

There was nothing in particular that Cathy did or didn't do. There were no shouting matches. She wasn't openly cruel. The passion just seemed to be slowly leaving the marriage. It broke Dan's heart but he seemed to be powerless to prevent it.

The state of the marriage didn't make him particularly look forward to going home but tonight he was dog tired.

When he arrived home, he found Cathy sitting in the living room with a stack of papers in front of her. He said "hey babe, what's up" and she said "I want out". Uncomprehending, he said "out of what". She said "our marriage". His jaw slowly dropped.

The stack of papers that Cathy had in front of her were the papers necessary to file for divorce and some related documentation. While he just stood there, dumbstruck, Cathy explained the content of the papers. Cathy explained that she just wanted out of the marriage and that money was not a big concern. She said that, if he would give her the house in which they were currently living, as well as $100,000, that was all that she wanted, materially. She told him that she had no interest in R and R accounting or any of the other assets that he had amassed over the years. She said "all you have to do is sign and walk away".

16

Dan took all of this in silently. He couldn't say a word. He knew that the passion had been slowly leaking out of the marriage for a long time but he had no idea that Cathy had become so unhappy that she would want a divorce and he certainly had no idea that she would have gone so far as to have had the papers drawn up.

Dan said "can't we talk about this?" Cathy said that she had no intention of talking about it and that she had her mind made up. She also said "if you fight me, it will become a lot more expensive for you", adding "I am asking for the house, which is probably worth 400 grand or so, plus another 100 thousand on top of that". She said "half of a million is quite reasonable for a man who is probably worth four or five million and you know, if I wanted, I could get half of it". Cathy said that the money wasn't what she cared about, she just wanted out, but that this was the only way that she knew of to get Dan to get on with the divorce, rather than trying to talk her out of it for a year.

Ultimately, Dan relented. A month later, he signed the divorce papers.

That night, he stayed in an apartment that he had rented that very day. He slept little, thinking about the failed marriage and trying to comprehend the reasons for it.

The biggest shadow that had fallen over the marriage was a lack of children. Had that been what had driven Cathy away? Had she somehow blamed him for that, even though numerous tests had shown that he was not the cause? Then again, those same tests had shown that she was not the cause either. Yet there had to be some cause. Perhaps children for them just wasn't meant to be.

Could it be that she had married him for money or at least the prospect of money and he hadn't satisfied her in that regard and so she had gone in search of greener pastures? He quickly dismissed that possibility. After all, he had ended up being more successful than either of them could have ever thought possible and she had only taken 10% when she could certainly have gotten 50%.

This thought brought Dan to yet another troubling thought. Cathy had given up at least two million just to expedite her departure from the marriage. Even if she was really unhappy, even if she wanted out, why was she in such a big hurry? Clearly, there was some piece to this puzzle that he hadn't found yet but, for the moment, he had grown too tired to think about it. Around midnight, he finally slept.

The next morning, Dan got up at 4:00am, unable to sleep any more. He showered, dressed, and headed to work. He had an appointment with his attorney, Gordon McDonald, at 10:00am to go ahead and sign the house over to Cathy and take care of a couple of other items, and he wanted to try to get some work done before that. He thought that working might help to get his mind off of his personal problems.

Dan's office was on the fifth floor. As he rode up in the elevator, he watched the floor indicator and his thoughts drifted back to the failed marriage. He tried to push it out of his mind, at least for the moment. After all, the reason that he was starting his work day three hours early was so that he could try to put Cathy out of his mind.

Dan went into the kitchen (there was one on each floor) and stared at the coffee machine. Dawn Anderson, his secretary, knew that he often came in early (though usually not this early) and that he liked his coffee first thing. Every evening, before she left, she put the coffee in the filter and the filter in the brew funnel so that all he had to do in the morning was push the brew button. He didn't ask her to do that. She was a very thoughtful person and she just did it to be helpful. All he had to do was push the little button but he just stood there, zoned out, for at least ten minutes, again thinking about Cathy. She would be getting up and taking a shower soon. He could smell the scent of her soap and shampoo drifting out of the bathroom along with the steam from her shower. What was she doing now? Why didn't she want him with her? And why in the heck was she in such a hurry to get rid of him? Was he really that bad? Oh crap! Who cares! He slapped the brew button and headed down the hall to his office.

Once Dan got into the work flow of the day, he did manage to push Cathy out of his mind or at least to the back of his mind.

As always, he checked his E-mail, first thing. He had an E-mail from Fred, reminding him to sign out the Staten project. Staten Floor Covering was a large floor covering retailer and one of R and R's larger clients. Carpet dealers were a dime a dozen in Georgia, probably because so much carpet was made there. Most of them weren't all that big but Staten was very large, with about 20 locations state wide. They had recently engaged R and R to do an audit and valuation. Most of the work was done by other people but all work done for clients as large as Staten had to be reviewed and signed out by a partner in the firm. Dan was the partner to which Staten was assigned. The completed audit and valuation had been ready for his review for three days but, like much of his work lately, he had let it slide.

The fact that Fred had E-mailed Dan about it suggested that someone had said something to Fred and he was probably wondering why Dan had to be prompted to get it signed out. It wasn't at all like Dan to let work just sit there. The reason that Dan had been letting things slide was because of his preoccupation with the situation with Cathy and himself. Fred didn't know about that yet. Dan had decided not to talk to Fred about the situation until after the divorce papers had been signed. Well, they had been signed and Gordon would be there at 10:00am to finalize everything so there was no reason to wait any longer. Dan sent Fred an E-mail, letting him know that he was about to sign out the Staten project and asking if Fred would be available for lunch at 11:00am, adding that there was a personal matter that he wanted to discuss.

19

Dan got out all of the Staten paperwork that Dawn had left on his desk three days prior and organized it. There was a considerable amount of it so this took several minutes. He took a trip down the hall to get his coffee and then he settled in to work. After he had been working for about thirty minutes, he heard the new E-mail chime from his computer. He turned around and looked at his screen. The E-mail was from Fred, sent from his iPhone, agreeing to the 11:00am lunch request. Dan was glad that this had been taken care of but he didn't want any more distractions so he closed the E-mail program on his computer and he went back to work. He became totally immersed in his work, which went smoothly. He had no interruptions other than when Dawn stuck her head in at 8:00am just to let him know that she was there. He finished the review at 9:45, just in time for his meeting with Gordon, and he E-mailed Fred to let him know that the review was done.

Gordon was always very prompt and today was no exception. Dawn ushered him into Dan's office promptly at 10:00am. Gordon was one of those people with enough energy to power a small city. He pumped Dan's hand vigorously and then plopped down, maintaining a constant string of small talk while he got out his laptop and unpacked some files from his briefcase onto his side of the desk. Then, down to business. He was leafing through the paperwork that he had gotten out. He was looking at it without really looking at it. He had checked it over ten times already and knew the contents by heart but this gave him something to do while he composed his thoughts. All at once, he plopped down the paperwork and sat back.

"Dan, I have got to say, there's something about this that troubles me."

"Well, it doesn't exactly make me happy."

Dan was being a smart aleck, which wasn't at all like him. Gordon hadn't caught Dan in the best of moods and Dan knew that he was being a jerk.

"Look, Gordon, I'm sorry. All of this just came at me out of the blue and I haven't been handling it all that great. I haven't slept well in a month. But, anyway, I'm sorry. What were you going to say?"

"No problem. If I were in your shoes, I don't think I would be handling it as well as you are. The thing that is bothering me is the divorce settlement or, to be more accurate, the lack of it. Cathy is asking for about half of a mil, give or take a little, and she could get much much more. I know that I am a lawyer, not an accountant, you are the accountant extraordinaire, but I have done a lot of estate planning work for you and, based on that, I know that your net worth is probably in the ballpark of five mil, maybe a little more. Now, of course, I'm your attorney and I'm on your side. It's great for you that she is leaving you with about 90% of your wealth but I have to ask myself why, when she could leave you with only 50% of it. It doesn't make sense and, when things like this don't make sense to me, it usually means that there is something about the situation that I don't know. Hidden facts can mean surprises down the road. I am an attorney and so I hate surprises. Is there anything here that you know that I need to know? You and I have done business for ten years. You know that I take client confidentiality very, very seriously."

"Yes, I do know that you take client confidentiality very seriously and, believe me, I am not worried about you blabbing. There is nothing else here that you need to know or, if there is, I don't know it either. I am just as puzzled as you are about the divorce settlement. I have thought about it for a month and I can't come up with anything."

"OK, well, if you think of anything, let me know. I have here the paperwork necessary to transfer complete ownership of the house to Cathy. That just leaves the hundred thousand. I have here a cashier's check that will take care of that. So, just a few signatures and you're done. Not much required to get rid of half a mil but, as I said, you are very fortunate that it isn't much more. I guess just sign,

21

count your blessings, and hope that there are no surprises on the horizon connected to this. But really though, even I can't imagine what kind of surprise there could be so you are probably fine."

Dan signed and Gordon packed up and left.

After Gordon left, Dan checked the time. It was 10:30am. Dan didn't have time to get started on anything else so he called Fred to see if he wanted to head to lunch early. Fred was free and said "good idea, I'm starving anyway, I didn't have breakfast". Fred came to Dan's office (it was just next door) and they talked for a minute about where they wanted to eat. Fred said "you know, I have been craving a good hamburger all week, how about Bob's Burger Barn". Dan wasn't really in the mood for a sit down lunch so he readily agreed. Bob's Burger Barn was about 30 minutes away and Dan thought a little drive would be nice so he suggested that he drive. Fred said "fine by me, let's go".

Dan drove a crew cab Chevrolet Silverado with a Duramax diesel under the hood. As he settled in behind the wheel and Fred got in, Fred, as usual, lamented Dan's choice of vehicle.

"Dan, when are you going to trade in this old clunker?"

"It isn't a clunker, it's only three years old and it's loaded."

"Well, it may be loaded and relatively new but it sounds like the pistons are swapping holes."

"Now, Fred, you know that all diesels sound like that."

"Yes, I know, which is why I would never own one. Why the heck would you buy a truck that rolls off the showroom floor sounding like it is about to fall apart?"

"I don't know, mostly, I guess, I like the way it sounds."

"Well, I like the way that my vette sounds better. Women like it too."

"Oh Fred, grow up."

This was an old argument between the two of them. Really, neither of them cared about what the other drove but they had this running argument ever since they had known each other, especially after R and R had really taken off and both of them could afford to buy whatever vehicle they wanted. Dan stuck with pickup trucks, which is what he had always liked. He kept a truck for years before trading it because he thought that getting a new one every year or two was just a waste of money and, even if you have money to burn, why would you if you don't have to? Fred saw things differently. Once he could afford it, Fred started driving a Corvette and he got a new one every year, always in a different color, probably so that people would notice that it wasn't the same one that he had the year before.

This said a lot about the differences in their character. Fred was always much more materialistic than Dan.

Dan never really chased the dollar. Sure, he wanted to make a good living, but it wasn't money that drove him. Enjoyment of hard work drove him. A sense of accomplishment drove him. That accomplishment did end up earning him some substantial wealth but that wasn't really the ultimate goal. He just worked his butt off and enjoyed every minute of it and then, one day, he basically looked around and said "hey, I have built up a little something". He was proud of it. Who wouldn't be? But he owned it, it didn't own him.

Now, Fred, on the other hand, was entirely driven by money. To be fair, his work ethic was every bit as tenacious as Dan's, maybe more so. However, the motivation for it was very different. When they started R and R accounting, Fred's stated goal was to become the richest man in Atlanta. He might have been well on his way to obtaining that goal by now if it weren't for one thing. He liked to spend money as well as he liked to earn it. At this point, Dan was worth five million or so. A little over half of that came from his share of R and R accounting and the rest came from various other investments that he had. Fred's net worth basically came from just his share of R and R because he always spent every penny that he can get his hands on. There was the Corvette, the house that was twice the size of Dan's and three times as expensive, the ski boat, and on and on.

So, basically, Dan was half as flashy but twice as wealthy, which Dan considered to be a good trade.

Once they got out of downtown Atlanta traffic, Dan decided to go ahead and raise the issue that he wanted to discuss. After all, they had a pretty good little drive ahead of them and he had rather discuss what he had to discuss in the cab of a truck with no one else around than discuss it in a diner that is so crowded that you could easily end up accidently salting your neighbor's fries instead of your own. Bob's had great food but it wasn't great for private conversation. Dan set the cruise control and began to compose his thoughts.

"Well, Fred, as I told you in that E-mail that I sent you this morning, I have something of a personal nature that I want to discuss. I think that I'll go ahead and get it out of the way now rather than waiting until we are eating at Bob's."

"Yeah, good idea. I can tell that something is eating at you lately and I doubt that it's just the fact that you drive a crappy truck."

Fred always was a smart aleck and usually Dan didn't mind. Really, he didn't mind even now because he figured that he could stand to lighten up a little after the month that he had had. Dan ignored the comment about his crappy truck and went ahead.

"OK, Fred, I'll just come right out with it. Cathy and I have split. She left me."

"Oh crap!"

He drew it out, "ooohhh cccrrraaappp".

"Dan, I'm sorry. You used the past tense. Is this already a done deal?"

"Yes, it's done. She told me that she wanted out a month ago, I signed the divorce papers yesterday, and Gordon brought the stuff for me to sign to get everything finalized this morning. I moved into a little apartment yesterday. That's why I left early. The moving wasn't difficult. I didn't take much and the apartment is furnished. Even though it is furnished, the apartment seems so empty, you know?"

"Well, I don't know how it is first hand but I can imagine. Man, that's tough. Things had been going downhill for a while, hadn't they?"

"Well, yeah, things hadn't really been good for a few years now but I didn't think that it would get to this point. Not yet anyway."

"Man, man, man. That really sucks."

They drove in silence for a while and then Fred spoke up.

"If you don't mind me asking, did she leave you anything?"

"Yeah, that may be the strangest thing about the whole mess. She left me almost everything. I signed over the house and wrote her a check for 100K and that's it."

"You're kidding! I couldn't get out of a divorce that cheap and you are probably worth quite a bit more than I am. I mean, it's great for you but very strange, you know?"

"Yeah, I know, Gordon and I had pretty much the same conversation this morning. For some darn reason, she was in a huge hurry to get the divorce done and behind. She used the fact that she could get a lot more money as leverage to get me to go ahead and sign the divorce papers. Darned if I know why she let me out so cheap and darned if I know why she was in such a big hurry but there you are."

When they got to Bob's Burger Barn, the place was packed. As small as it was, it would have been packed with ten people and there were probably five times that. That was just part of the atmosphere though and you got use to it if you ate there often, which they both did. They mostly ate in silence. The atmosphere wasn't really conducive to conversation and Dan didn't feel like talking anyway.

When they started back, they drove in silence for about ten minutes. Then Fred spoke.

"Man that was good! Hey, wasn't that where you met Cathy?"

"Yes it was. Nice of you to bring it up."

"Oh, sorry man, wasn't thinking."

"That's OK, you're just a jerk at heart anyway."

They both laughed and then they drove in silence a bit longer. Fred spoke again.

"I guess, for you, Atlanta is full of memories, of you and Cathy I mean ."

"Here you go again, Mr. jerk."

"Well, I'm just saying, it would drive me nuts. Then again, this whole thing would drive me nuts. If you need anything or just want to talk, my office is right next door and you know my number and where I live. Call on me any time."

"Thanks, I will."

That night, Dan lay in bed in his tiny, furnished yet empty apartment. He lay in the dark and listened to the sounds of the emptiness. From the bed, he could hear the refrigerator kick on and off because the kitchen was right next door to the only bedroom. It had just started to get cool enough that a little heat at night was needed in order to be comfortable. Dan could hear the sound of the heated air blowing through the vents in the ceiling of the bedroom. It made a soft whish sound. There was little traffic but there was the sound of the occasional car going by and, in the distance, a dog was barking.

He kept thinking back to what Fred had said about how living in Atlanta with all of the memories would drive him nuts. Truthfully, it had only been a month since all this started and it was already driving Dan nuts. He ate at Bob's Burger Barn about once a week and, every time he did, he thought about Cathy sitting on that stool that first day and all of their dates there in the years that followed, talking about everything in the world and usually going to a movie afterward. Every day, on his way to work, he passed the church where he and Cathy were married and his thoughts would drift back to that beautiful flowing white wedding gown and the even more beautiful woman within it. She was absolutely radiant. Dan had actually shed a tear when he saw her that day and he was not a crying man. Oh, how everything had changed.

Oh yes, Atlanta was driving him crazy but what could he do about it? Surely, in time, it would get better. And, anyway, what

27

could he do about it? Where could he go? He had business
connections all over the country but the only other place where he
had family and friends was Jackson, Tennessee. Going back home
and trying to start over was crazy! Wasn't it? What about R and R?
Yes, crazy! Absolutely nuts! He admonished himself to stop all this
foolishness and, exhausted, he rolled over and went to sleep.
However, the seed had been planted.

Chapter 3

April 1, 2013

That seed eventually flowered. In March, Dan sold his share of R and R Accounting. He was now sitting here, this early April morning, about to leave Atlanta for Jackson. He was really doing it. At forty years old, he was dropping everything that he had worked for and starting over, in a place that was old yet new to him. He found the prospect of what lay ahead both saddening and exciting. He was saddened by the life that could have been for him and Cathy, now lost forever. On the other hand, he had to admit to himself that the marriage had not been in good shape for quite a while and, in the long run, he might even be better off. This thought was in the very back of his mind but it was there as he got up and prepared to leave the tiny apartment for the last time.

When Dan arrived at R and R accounting, he parked in his usual place, one of four parking slots that had been reserved for the four partners, of which there were now only three. He got out of his truck and, as he walked to the front door, he surveyed the building. It was an impressive five story structure, fronted mostly by glass. The first floor contained a large and plush reception area at the front of the building with four large conference rooms at the rear. The second, third, and fourth floors contained the offices of the associate CPAs and most of the clerical support staff. The fifth floor contained the offices of the partners and their clerical support staff, including their personal secretaries. R and R accounting had purchased the building five years ago. At the time, it was a bit larger than the firm really needed but R and R had continued to experience explosive growth and had quickly grown into it. As he looked at the building, Dan felt a rush of pride at having been one of the driving forces behind that growth.

He came in and waved to Teresa, the main receptionist, who was on the phone at the moment. He boarded the elevator and pressed the button for the fifth floor. He was glad that Teresa had been on the phone and that the elevator was empty. Now that the time had come to go, he didn't want to spend all day saying goodbye. He stepped off of the elevator and headed for his office. He waved to Dawn, who was on the phone, went into his office, and shut the door.

He sat down in his chair. He surveyed the room; the huge desk which was now void of its usual clutter of papers, the wall of glass behind the desk, the leather side chairs in front of it. He looked to his left at the floor to ceiling built in cherry book case, filled with volumes related to all kinds of accounting and general business topics. Dawn would be packing those up and shipping them to him in Jackson. He looked to his right at the leather sofa with cherry trunk style end tables and lamps with broad column like cherry bases. At the moment, those lamps were the only lights on and the heavy scarlet colored drapes were drawn across the wall of glass, lending a warm glow to the room.

Dawn had been mostly responsible for the decor. By the time that the building had been purchased, Cathy had mostly lost interest in R and R. Dan knew that he certainly didn't have the sense of style needed to do it and hiring an expensive decorator seemed like a waste of money. He had asked Dawn to take care of it and she had happily agreed. She said that she had once wanted to become a decorator and that she really enjoyed the little project. Dan certainly thought that she had done a very good job and for relatively little money.

Fred had hired someone to design and decorate his office. It had cost three times as much as Dan's office, not counting the fees of the decorator, and Dan thought that his own office looked much better; more comfortable, more warm and inviting.

There was a knock at the door. Dan called "come in" in a voice that was more cheerful than he felt. The door opened and Dawn stood there, looking a bit tentative.

"Mr. Richardson, am I disturbing you?"

"It's Dan, not Mr. Richardson, especially considering that you no longer work for me, and no, you are not disturbing me. Come in."

She came in and sat in one of the side chairs. She was 30 years old, relatively slender, about 5'6", with a fair complexion, bluish green eyes, and shoulder length blond hair that was currently in a ponytail. She was dressed in jeans and a shirt which said "Go Braves". She normally dressed much more formally but, in the last couple days, she had dressed very casually because she had been helping Dan to clean his office and pack up his things so she wanted to wear something that would be comfortable and that wouldn't matter if it got dirty. Dan had always thought that she was very attractive. Not the kind of beauty that screams "look at me" but a quiet beauty that would probably still be there in twenty or thirty years.

"Mr. Richardson, Dan, I just want to tell you how great it has been working for you all of these years. It just won't be the same without you."

"That is very flattering of you to say. I know that there were times when I wasn't all that pleasant to work for, especially in the last few months. In fact, I know that I have really been a jerk lately. I'm sorry about that. You didn't deserve to have to deal with the person who I had become lately. I hope that you can forgive me for that."

"No apology is necessary and there is nothing to forgive. I am so sorry about what Cathy did to you. She didn't know what she had. You are the nicest guy in this entire building. Before the whole mess with Cathy, you were a little quiet but always very friendly. Look at what you did for Rob and me when he lost his job."

"Well, you and Rob were having a hard time. You needed the money more than I did. Anyone fortunate enough to have had my resources would have done the same thing."

"Now, see, that's what I'm talking about. That ten thousand dollars saved us, financially, and you are too much of a nice guy to even take credit for it. Do you think that the other cofounder next door would have done that?"

Dan laughed nervously.

"Well, no, probably not."

"Probably not heck. You know darned well that he wouldn't have. Not ten thousand, not one thousand, not one hundred."

"I had it. I didn't need it. You are one heck of an employee and you did need it so I gave it to you and I was quite happy to do it. Case closed."

Dawn stood and so did Dan. She came around the desk and gave him a sustained bear hug. When she drew back, she had tears in her eyes. With her hands resting lightly on his shoulders, in a quavering voice, she said "I was lucky to have had a boss like you and someday some woman will be lucky to have a man like you, Cathy is an idiot". She hugged him again quickly and disengaged.

Dan got choked up himself and, at the moment, he felt better than he had in months.

"Well, I don't quite know what to say. Thank you Dawn. I will truly miss you and I wish you and Rob all the best. If either of you need anything, just let me know. By the way, are you OK now financially? Rob has been working for a while now but he was out of work for a really long time. Two years wasn't it? Do you need more money? I mean, it's really no bother if you do. Unfortunately, I never had any children to spend my money on and I no longer have a wife. Heck, someone may as well benefit from all of these years of work."

Dawn's previously unshed tears now ran down her face but, fortunately, today there was no make-up for them to smear.

"No, we're fine now. Anyway, you better hang on to that money. I have a feeling that you will end up having both a wife and kids to spend it on, some day. I'm going to go now before I turn into a blubbering idiot."

She hugged him again quickly and was gone.

Dan sat back down. The conversation with Dawn had really buoyed his spirits. Ever since Cathy had left him, he had felt like there had to be something wrong with him because she hadn't been happy being married to him and because, for some unknown reason, she was in such a hurry to get away from him. It also made him feel like no woman would ever want him. Dawn had made him see that maybe he wasn't such a bad guy and, perhaps, there could be happiness in his future after all.

One thing was certain. If he ever did have a wife and children, he would be able to provide well for them. Three months ago, he had told Fred that he wanted out of R and R accounting. The painful memories that were associated with Atlanta just kept surfacing more and more often, especially at Christmas time, when everyone else seemed to be so happy. The day after new years, Dan came in and told Fred that he just had to get away from Atlanta. Dan had thought that Fred would try to talk him out of it and he did, a little, but not as strenuously as Dan had expected. Fred had said that he understood, which was a relief to Dan because he didn't want to spend months convincing Fred that this was what he was going to do, come hell or high water.

They had set up a meeting in mid-January to discuss the situation with the other partners. Dan and Fred, as the founding partners, had previously each retained 30% of the firm, while the other two partners each had a 20% share. It was decided that Dan's portion would now be bought out by the other three partners in such a manner that they would all have equal one-third shares.

They had to arrange a formal valuation of R and R accounting. Corporate valuations were performed on a regular basis by R and R but of course it would have been a conflict of interest for R and R to do a valuation of itself. With the blessing of the other partners, Dan had called his old friend, Mike Hannon, founder of Hannon and Associates, in Jackson, Tennessee. Hannon and Associates wasn't nearly as big as R and R but it was more than up to the task of competently handling a large corporate valuation.

The valuation took about a week. One day, in the middle of it, Mike invited Dan to lunch. He was a little concerned about Dan and how he was handling the divorce. For one thing, he felt that Dan's decision to sell his share of R and R was perhaps ill advised and was certainly made with too much haste. Mike thought that perhaps he could get Dan to at least consider the situation a little more carefully before acting. About half way through lunch, after a lot of small talk, Mike brought the conversation around to Dan's decision to sell his share of R and R.

"I must say, Dan, I am surprised at your decision to sell."

"really?"

"You have spent so much time and effort building the business and you always seemed to love your work so much."

"I do still enjoy the work but I am getting a little tired of the drudgery. I guess I'm getting a little burned out."

"I can understand that. This business can certainly do that. I feel a little burned out from time to time myself. It helps if you have some interests outside the business. Do you have anything outside of R and R that you enjoy? Anything that you're passionate about?"

"No, not really. The two things that I was passionate about were the business and Cathy. I got tired of the business and Cathy got tired of me. So, I guess there go all my passions."

Dan laughed.

"Look Mike, you are starting to depress me. Enough about my life. What about you? What are you passionate about?"

"Well, outside of the business, the only thing that I am really active in is church."

"Church? You are passionate about that? I'm sorry. I don't mean to sound condescending. You are a awesome guy but you just don't strike me as a religious man.

"I am not there absolutely every time that the door is open but I am there most of the time and I teach a Sunday school class."

"I've never been very churchy. I just never could get into it. I believe in God. I have read the Bible some and I try to be a good person. That's what you do in church, right? Study the Bible and try to learn how to be a better person? I guess I just never thought that church would help me with that very much. I mean, don't get me wrong, I don't think I'm perfect but it seems to me that I'm doing alright at being a good person on my own."

Mike was troubled. What Dan had said bothered him. Clearly, Dan was not a Christian. Mike was a Christian but what kind of Christian was he? Dan didn't see him as a religious man? How long had Mike known Dan? About 20 years? And, in all that time, the subject of Dan's faith or lack of it had never come up? Another

35

thing that bothered him was his own indecisiveness concerning how to respond. He had attended church regularly and even taught Sunday school for years but he had never been a very bold witness. He could teach people about God in a room full of people who had come to learn about Him but this was different. Faced with the prospect of defending his church attendance and his faith to someone who probably didn't really want to hear it, he didn't know what to do or what to say. He had planned to ask Dan if he had prayed about his decision but, the way the conversation was going, he didn't think there was much point in it. Mike felt shame at his indecisiveness and inadequacy and he did the only thing that he could think of. He changed the subject and he didn't say much for the rest of the meal.

It was determined that the total value of R and R Accounting was 10.3 million dollars, which meant that Dan's 30% share was worth almost 3.1 million. The restructuring was easiest on Fred. Because he already owned almost one-third, he only had to come up with a little over 300K. However, the other two partners had to come up with almost 1.4 million each. All three of them borrowed against the stock that they were buying and, between that and their other financial interests, it wasn't a problem.

On March 21, all of the partners signed the necessary paperwork and Dan was presented with a cashier's check in the amount of $3,090,000.

As Dan sat there, it was comforting to know that, whatever the future held, he was financially secure. He took one last look around the room and decided that he had already gotten everything that really mattered. Dawn could send him the rest later. He got up, turned out the lights, and left his office.

Dan took a few steps down the hall and knocked on the open door of Fred's office. Dan said "I'm out of here". Fred came around the desk, shook Dan's hand, and said "good luck buddy". Dan said "thanks" and he turned around and started down the hall toward the elevator.

Right after Dan left Fred's office, Fred stood there, in the doorway of his office, and watched Dan recede down the hall. As soon as Dan got to the elevator, Fred closed the door. He sat down behind his desk and took an index card from the lap drawer. He picked up the telephone and dialed the number on the card. When the person on the other end answered, Fred said "he's on his way". The other person said "excellent" and they hung up.

Chapter 4

On the way out of town, Dan decided to stop at Bob's Burger Barn one last time for breakfast. Because of the memories of Cathy that intruded every time that he ate there, he had avoided the place for months. But, darn it, the food was good! Besides, he was feeling better today and he thought that it might be less painful this time. He came in and took the same seat at the counter that he had taken the day that he met Cathy. He ordered a large stack of pancakes, bacon, eggs, hash browns, and coffee. He ate a large breakfast because, other than the occasional bathroom stop, he planned to drive strait through to Jackson. As he ate, he thought back over the morning that he had had. It hadn't started out all that well but the latter part of the morning had been rather nice. The memories weren't quite so painful this time and that made him feel even better. Yes, maybe everything was going to be OK after all. He paid the check, used the bathroom, and went out the door whistling. He got in his truck, turned on his favorite CD, and thought "Jackson, here I come".

Dan drove straight through from Atlanta to Jackson, only stopping twice to use the bathroom and once for fuel. The trip took about eight hours and, as he pulled off of the interstate, he was very hungry and dog tired.

As Dan pulled into his parents' driveway, he just wanted a good hot meal, a shower, and a nice warm bed. He turned off the key of his truck and blew out an exhalation of relief that his journey was finally over. When the clatter of the diesel engine ceased, the sudden quiet seemed strange after so many hours of hearing the constant drone. He just sat there for a few minutes and let the quiet and his own fatigue wash over him. He had to admit to himself that, even with his fatigue and hunger after the long trip, he felt surprisingly good. After so many years of work, work, work, it might feel good to slow down a little. He also felt an optimism about the future that he hadn't felt in a long time and that felt really good. He was starting to think that coming back home to Jackson really had been the right idea.

He got out of the truck and headed for the door. As he passed through the garage, he patted the trunk of his mother's gray 2003 Chevrolet Impala and looked over at his father's white 2004 crew cab Chevrolet Silverado, which, accept for the color, was almost identical to Dan's, including the Duramax diesel engine. Neither of Dan's parents had ever been into flashy vehicles, although they could have certainly afforded to drive whatever they wanted.

Dan knocked on the door, which was opened almost immediately by his mother. Ramona Richardson looked good for her age of 63 years. She was relatively short, about 5'2", and a bit plump but not terribly overweight. She had short, gray almost white hair. Her eyes were green and very bright and warm. If you were her husband or her children, those eyes could make you feel like you were the most wonderful thing on earth which, to her, you were. If she felt that you were a threat to her children or her husband, those eyes could project a penetrating laser directly into the depths of your soul and freeze it solid. At the moment, she wore a light blue shirt just like Dan's with the R and R Accounting logo emblazoned in red on the front, jeans, and tennis shoes, also just like Dan. Wafting out the door around her was what may have been the most delicious aroma that Dan had ever smelled.

She enveloped Dan in a vice like sustained bear hug. Just when he thought that he would pass out from lack of circulation, she pulled back to arm's length, looked up into his face, and bare hugged him again. She disengaged from him, slapped him on the arm, and said "well, are you going to stand there or are you going to come in here", as she turned away from the door and called out "Gary, Dan is here". Oh yes, it was good to be home.

Dan followed her into the kitchen, where the heavenly aroma intensified.

40

"I am absolutely starving and I think that is the most wonderful thing that I have ever smelled. What is it?"

"It's country fried steak, mashed potatoes, black eyed peas, fried okra, and a dessert that you will find out about when you see it. It isn't ready yet. It will be about half an hour or so. Now get out of my kitchen so I can finish. Go and talk to your father for a while. He is very anxious to see you. I will bring the two of you coffee in a few minutes."

"Oh yes, coffee sounds almost as good as the food that you are cooking. I am dog tired and I could use some caffeine."

"Good, now get."

About this time, Gary came into the kitchen. Like his wife, he had gray hair, almost white. He was about 5'9", a couple inches shorter than Dan, and he had a bit of a pudgy stomach but, in general, he was in good shape, especially for a man of 65. His eyes were gray and they peered from behind stylish, thin framed glasses. His eyes did not belie his emotions as did the eyes of his wife. He was wearing a light green polo shirt and black slacks. He delivered a bear hug similar to that of Ramona and led Dan down the hall to his study.

Coincidentally, Gary's study looked similar to Dan's office. There was a large oak desk with a large, high back, leather office chair behind it and two leather side chairs in front of it. On the wall behind the desk were several windows, over which the blinds were currently closed. Parallel to one side of the desk was a bookshelf that took up an entire wall, filled with many volumes, ranging from law books to novels. On the opposite wall was a leather sofa with two oak end tables, on which rested two large lamps. These lamps were providing the only light in the room. On the desk rested a closed laptop computer, a few papers, and a small stack of books. Sitting in this room reminded Dan of sitting in his office that morning in Atlanta.

"I really like this study. It reminds me a lot of my former office in Atlanta. How long did it take you to convince mom to turn it from her living room into your study?"

"Oh, not too long. We very rarely used the formal living room anyway. We have always spent most of our time in the kitchen and the den and that is where we usually entertain guests when we have them, which isn't often."

"How long have you had it, the study I mean?"

"Well, I guess it has been about two years. As you know, I retired about three years ago but I have continued to provide consulting services to other attorneys in the area. Not much, just a few hours per week, but it was not convenient not to have my own work space. At first, I was going to put it upstairs. It made sense to me because that big room up there isn't used for anything anyway and it has a separate heating and cooling unit which I could have kept turned off when I wasn't using it. Your mother wouldn't hear of it."

Gary affected a high pitched voice and, attempting to imitate Ramona, said "Gary, at your age, you have no business traipsing up and down those stairs all of the time".

From the door, Ramona said "and I was right too".

Gary grudgingly said "well, maybe", and he chuckled.

Ramona placed large, steaming mugs of black coffee in front of each of them and left.

Gary said "anyway, if we had turned that upstairs room into a study, where would you stay now".

Dan said "good point" and laughed.

Father and son sat for a few minutes and sipped their coffee in silence. Then, Gary spoke.

"Well, Dan, I must say that when you first told me that you were selling your share of R and R accounting and coming back to Jackson, I thought that you were being very foolish. I thought that, because of Cathy, you were running away from Atlanta and, in the process, walking away from a whole lot of additional potential wealth."

"You not only thought it, you said it, very plainly."

"Yes I did. You know that I have never been one to mince words."

"Well, more and more, I believe that it was the right decision."

"I suppose that remains to be seen. What are your plans anyway?"

"Well, first of all, I guess I will need to look for a house."

"You know that you are welcome to stay here for as long as you like."

"Yes, I know, and I appreciate it."

"But?"

"But you know that, in short order, mom will be minding my business and telling me all of the reasons why what I am planning won't work. I love her to death but that just drives me nuts."

"Yeah, in the early days, she didn't have much faith in my ability to build a successful law practice either but here I am retired with more money than I know what to do with."

"I have already demonstrated my own ability to build wealth and you would think that she could take the past as evidence of future potential."

Gary sat back in his chair.

"Speaking of building wealth, what are your plans in that regard?"

"I plan on sort of starting over. I think I will open a little one man shop and contract out CFO services to businesses that are too small to have full time CFOs. I think I could do well with something like that."

"You might be able to make a living doing that but I don't think that you will ever build substantial wealth doing it, certainly not the kind of wealth that you built with R and R."

"Well, at this point, earning a living is all that I really need to do. I don't have to build substantial wealth. I already have substantial wealth. Between the money from selling my share of R and R and what I already had in the bank, I have about three and a half million in cash. I also have a couple million in commercial real estate in Atlanta, which is netting about 15K per month so, really, I don't even have to earn a living. I'm just looking for something to do. You know that I could never stand to just sit on my rear but I'm tired of the day to day drudgery of working at R and R. I want something challenging and maybe even a little exciting. Is that too much to ask?"

Before Gary could answer, Ramona's voice floated down the hall from the kitchen, "come and get it".

Dan was ravenous and he hadn't had his mother's wonderful cooking in years. He ate two plates full. For dessert, she had made his favorite, chocolate chess pie, and he had a huge piece. They all sat around the table and talked for a little while and then Dan excused himself to go to bed early.

He went out to his truck and got his suit case that contained his toiletries and a couple changes of clothes. He decided that he could get the rest tomorrow. He warily pushed open the double doors that led to the second floor and slowly trudged up the stairs. His legs felt like they were made of lead.

At the top of the stairs, to the left, was a bathroom. To the right was a large square room, about 30'x 30', which contained a twin size bed, a queen size bed, a old living room suit, a big screen TV, a piano, a small antique roll top desk, and a small book case. The floor was carpeted but with the mishmash of random items, the room looked almost like someone's attic.

On the far wall, where the living room suit sat, just above the couch, was a thermostat that controlled the heating and cooling unit for the room, which was independent from the heating and cooling for the rest of the house. Dan turned the temperature setting down to 65 degrees. He liked it cool when he slept. He brushed his teeth, stripped down to his underwear, and collapsed into the queen size bed, which his mother had turned down for him, just as she had done when he was a child. He groggily thought "it sure is nice to be home". He fell asleep immediately and he slept better than he had in six months.

Chapter 5

As Dan was going to sleep, Cathy sat in the living room of Ben Nelson, her fiancé. She was working on her laptop computer, composing an E-mail. Ben was standing behind the sofa on which she sat, looking over her shoulder at the laptop screen, reading the message that she was composing.

From: Cathy Richardson

To: Jake Richardson

Subject: Company Working on Cure for Blindness

Jake,

I hope that you are doing well and I hope that you don't think badly of me after what has happened between Dan and me. I would like to hope that I can remain friends with the Richardson family, especially you, as I have always admired your strength and perseverance. I was just surfing the web and I ran across the website of a biotech company that is working to cure blindness. Given what I know about your eye condition, I think that the technology that this company is working on may be able to help you. The name of the company is Vision Biotech. Their website is www.visionbiotech.com. Check it out. They are located right here in Memphis so, if you like what you read on the site, you might want to contact them and find out if they will see you. I hope that they can help you.

Take Care,

Cathy

Cathy looked up at Ben and asked "what do you think".

"Well, you might want to change 'right here in Memphis' to something like 'just down the road in Memphis'. Remember, he doesn't know that you are in Memphis and we don't want him to know."

Cathy smacked herself in the forehead with the heel of her hand.

"Oh crap! I wasn't thinking."

She made the suggested change and said "now what do you think".

"Looks good to me."

"Do you want me to send it?"

"Yes."

She clicked the send button and then shut down the laptop, closed it, and sat it on the coffee table. Ben came around the back of the sofa and sat down beside her.

Cathy looked at him appraisingly. He was about 6'1" or 6'2", about 210 pounds, with short, black hair. He had steely gray eyes that peered out from behind large framed glasses. He hadn't changed since coming home from work and he was currently wearing a light gray button down shirt with a white lab coat on over it and black slacks. He basically looked like the nerd that he was but those gray eyes could sometimes project a coldness that she found a little disconcerting.

He asked "do you think this will work".

She thought for a minute before she spoke.

"Well, yes, I think that this will get Jake to Memphis and, yes, I think that Dan will come with him, especially given the timing. Dan and Jake have always been close and they haven't seen much of each other in years so they will probably want to spend some time together now. Dan bringing Jake to an appointment with Vision Biotech would be an excellent opportunity to do that. From there, it's going to be up to you to get Dan on board."

"Oh, if he comes and I show him what I could do for his brother if I were to have the right source of funding, I can get him on board. No question."

"I do feel a little bad, using Jake to get to Dan like this. I really have always liked and respected Jake."

"Cathy, do you hear what you're saying? Using him? Well, OK, I guess we are technically using him, a little, but look what he gets in return? He can have his vision back. Not just back but better than it ever was."

"And you are sure of that?"

"Oh yes, absolutely, without a doubt. Cathy, I'm telling you, this technology that we are working on is one of the holy grails of medicine. A cure to blindness! Not only will I be able to bring sight to your brother-in-law, and thousands like him, but I will make us rich beyond anything that you can possibly imagine. I just have to get beyond these capital problems and Dan can help me to do that. The money that you let go in the divorce will be multiplied thousands of times over, once it has been invested with Vision Biotech."

"This is how you were talking back when you first started getting money from that, um, shall we say less than reputable source."

Ben's eyes were suddenly infused with that coldness that Cathy found so disconcerting. He spoke in a low voice.

"Don't you ever mention that again. I don't even know why I told you about that. If you start blabbing, you will get all of us put away for twenty years."

Cathy's heart skipped a beat. Right now, she not only found the coldness in his eyes disconcerting, she found it a bit frightening. She had a feeling that he could be dangerous, if he were pushed too far or backed into a corner. She tread carefully.

"Ben, I haven't blabbed to anyone and I'm not going to. If you go to prison, my future goes down the drain. I have invested everything in this plan to save Vision Biotech and, if you lose, I lose too. I didn't mean to imply that I don't have faith in you or Vision Biotech. It's just that, with everything on the line, I get nervous."

She reached out and softly took his hand. His face softened. When he spoke again, it was with a calmer voice.

"Did you close on the house in Atlanta last week? I have been so busy, I forgot to ask."

"Yes, I closed on the house last week and I sent Fred a check today, after he called me and told me that Dan was on his way."

"How much did you settle on?"

"I gave him 400 thousand, which is more than it cost him to buy his portion of Dan's portion of R and R but I am hoping that the extra will help to keep him quiet. I don't like having to deal with him. He is very smart and he is driven purely by greed and people like that can be dangerous to deal with."

"That's true. However, we needed him to encourage Dan to come back to this area. Given what you have told me about Dan, without a little push, I'm not at all sure that he would have ever left Atlanta. Also, Fred was invaluable in getting the other partners to agree to the buyout of Dan's portion and then helping to set

50

everything up. All things considered, I think that what we paid for his assistance was a very good deal."

"Maybe but he still makes me nervous."

What Cathy thought but didn't say was that Fred wasn't the only person who made her nervous. Ben did too.

A little over a year ago, Ben had come to Atlanta to attend a biotech conference and that was when she had met him. They had both eaten lunch at the same restaurant and had started talking while each of them was waiting on a table. He had swept her off of her feet. He was the founder of a biotech startup which was working to cure blindness. The company promised to be a pioneer in its field. It also promised to, if successful, make Ben the wealthiest man in the United States or, perhaps, the wealthiest man in the world. She found him to be very exciting, in contrast to Dan who worked hard but who in the end was just a bean counter, albeit a very successful one.

When she had met Dan, she had seen how ambitious that he was and that he had laid a good foundation on which to nurture that ambition into actual accomplishment. Dan had eventually become wealthy. He had money but he didn't care about using that money to gain influence or power. He was content to work away, day after day, in the same old drudgery. He was continually earning more and more money but Cathy had come to understand that it was not the money that drove him. He was driven by a love of his work and a sense of accomplishment. To Dan, the money seemed to just be an incidental byproduct of work. He didn't care about fancy cars, just look at his truck. He didn't care about a big house. Fred's house was much bigger and nicer. She knew that, if Fred could have the fancy cars and the big house, then so could Dan but he just didn't place much value in material possessions.

She wanted something more. She didn't just want money. She wanted excitement. She wanted power and influence. Maybe that would help to fill the void within her. Ben didn't yet have all that much money but he loved influence and power. Cathy thought that he would be a very exciting man to be with if he ever did acquire the money and status that would afford him influence and power. She thought that he was on the way up and she wanted to ride along with him.

Cathy and Ben had started an affair. She had arranged to see him a couple times while he was in Atlanta, attending the biotech conference. They had exchanged phone numbers and E-mail addresses and, after Ben went back home to Memphis, they began to communicate more and more often. Initially, they would just correspond by E-mail. Just a couple times per week, at first, and gradually the frequency of the E-mails had increased to daily and then multiple times per day. Then, they had begun to communicate by telephone.

Ben did most of the talking and Cathy was content to let him. He talked about all of the strides that he was making and was about to make in his work. He talked about how close he was to realizing his ultimate goal. He talked about how, once that was accomplished, he was going to take the company public. He talked about all of the money that was going to come pouring in. He talked about how he was on the way to the top and how he was going to take Cathy to the top right along with him. He talked and he talked and he talked. He really seemed to believe everything that he was saying and he made her believe it too.

At first, the relationship had not been physical. On the occasions when they had met, during the biotech conference, they had simply had dinner and talked. Then, for a couple months, they just communicated by E-mail and phone. One day, she had gotten an E-mail from him, saying that he was going to be in Atlanta again, to meet with a supplier of a product that would be used in the next phase of his work. He said that he wanted to see her again and asked if she could arrange it.

Cathy didn't hesitate. She knew that meeting Ben wouldn't pose a problem. Dan worked twelve hours most days and he wasn't at all the suspicious type. It would never occur to him to check up on what she had done during the day. Even if an acquaintance of Dan saw Cathy and Ben out somewhere and they mentioned it to Dan, she could give him some offhanded explanation and he would accept it without question. In fact, she knew that, if she wanted, she could have Ben meet her right there, in her and Dan's house, and it wouldn't be a problem. As it turned out, that is exactly what happened.

Ben came over for lunch. She had made salads and they grilled steaks. They ate on the back patio. The back yard was surrounded by a six foot wooden privacy fence so she wasn't worried about the neighbors seeing them and, even if that happened, she knew that she could handle Dan. They each drank several glasses of wine and, with their inhibitions lowered, eventually, one thing led to another.

Thus began the physical part of the affair. In the next few months, Ben was in Atlanta three more times, on business, and, each time, he and Cathy got together for a little tryst, always in Dan's house, always in Dan's bed. The daily E-mails and phone calls continued as well.

Ben had been fascinated when he had found out that Cathy's brother-in-law was blind and that he had an eye condition that was treatable by the technology that Ben's company was working on. At first, Ben seemed to just have professional interest in Jake, seeing him only as a potential candidate for treatment, someone who could be used to help develop the technology in clinical trials. However, then, when Vision Biotech started having financial problems, Ben had started talking about using Jake in order to get Dan to invest in his company.

By this time, Cathy had begun talking about leaving Dan for Ben. She and Ben created a plan to lure Dan into investing in Vision Biotech. The plan was for Cathy to leave Dan with almost all of his wealth so that he would have all of it to invest in Vision Biotech. Then, when he did so, she would get all of his wealth, not just half of it, plus the incalculable rewards that would come from the success of Vision Biotech. The only thing that she would take in the Divorce was the house and a little cash, which would be used to pay Fred for his part. She had no doubt but what Fred would cooperate because, in the deal, he would basically get a bigger stake in R and R accounting and it would cost him nothing. So far, everything was going according to plan.

Still, Cathy was nervous. Everything had been set in motion. She had played her part and, really, Ben didn't need her any more. Not financially anyway. She had begun to wonder if financial interest was the only interest that he had had in her. Could that be true? If so then she had even more reason to fear that coldness in his eyes.

Ben spoke.

"One thing does worry me about this plan."

"What's that? "

"Well, the plan is to get Dan interested in what I can do for Jake and then recruit him to be the chief financial officer (CFO), so that he can see for himself the financial condition of the company without me having to tell him. He will be distraught when he sees that, without an infusion of capital, the company will not survive and, if the company does not survive, his brother will not benefit from the technology that we are developing."

"Yes, I know that. I helped to come up with the plan, remember?"

"Yes, I know, I know. Just hang on for a second. You have said that Dan has extensive training and experience in forensic accounting, correct?"

"Yes, he is certified in forensic accounting."

"Well, you see, I find that troubling. The reason that Vision Biotech has survived this long is the capital from that less than reputable funding source that you mentioned."

"I'm sorry that I mentioned that."

"That's OK, just listen. I am fearful that, with Dan's training and experience, he will stumble onto something that will make him suspicious. If that were to happen, he might not invest or, worse, he might disclose his suspicions to law enforcement. That is something that we do not need, not when I am this close to grabbing the brass ring."

"Ben, I told you. Dan is not a hard man to deceive. I did it for years. He and I were married for fourteen years and he never really knew me. Besides, even if he was to be suspicious, he couldn't prove anything, could he?"

"I don't know. I doubt it. Don't underestimate him though. He may not have figured you out but he couldn't perform an audit on your soul. He can and probably will perform an audit on the books of Vision Biotech, especially given that we hope to go public in relatively short order. I really don't think that he will find anything but it still worries me."

"Oh, it will be fine. You worry too much. Come with me to bed and I will make you forget all about your worries."

"Well, OK, you talked me into it."

They got up and headed down the hall for the bedroom. Just outside the door, Ben turned around and faced her.

"Cathy?"

"Yes?"

"You aren't playing me, are you? The way that you played Dan?"

That coldness returned to his eyes and her blood ran just as cold.

"No, of course not."

"Good."

He held her gaze for a moment and then he turned and went into the bedroom.

Chapter 6

The next morning, at 6:00am, Jake's bedroom sounded like the inside of a bell tower, which is the alarm tone that he had chosen for his wake up alarm. He reached over to his iPhone and touched the bottom of the screen. The phone said "slide to stop alarm". He double tapped and the alarm fell silent.

He lay there for a few minutes, thinking about the day ahead. He was very glad that Dan was now going to be living in Jackson and he felt sure that Dan would be coming by to visit with him later in the day.

He was looking forward to being able to spend time with Dan, something that he had not been able to do, accept on very rare occasions, in years. He hoped that, by spending some time together, they would be able to get to know each other a little better.

Jake had always felt that most people, including most of his family, did not really know him. Unfortunately, this included Dan. Dan had always been very supportive of Jake, always willing to help out however he could. Most of Dan's help had been financial as he had lived too far away to do anything else but the financial assistance that he provided was very generous. In fact, he had purchased the house in which Jake now lived. Jake certainly could not claim any lack of support and he truly appreciated all that Dan had done for him.

However, Jake had always felt that Dan's perception of him was not accurate. Of course, Jake was disabled. No one, including Jake, would argue otherwise. However, Dan's perception of him was defined too much by that disability. Dan saw him as being less capable and more limited than he really was. He even felt that Dan saw him as being a bit childlike.

Jake knew that blind people did, of course, have many limitations that people with normal eyesight did not have. However, he also knew that blind people were capable of many things and he felt that many of their limitations were self-imposed. Dan did not think that blind people were totally helpless but he did not understand Jake's attitude. It wasn't that he just disagreed with Jake's point of view but, rather, he literally did not understand what Jake's point of view was, though he thought that he did, and this was very frustrating to Jake.

Dan had once told Jake "you think that you have no limitations". Jake had never felt that way and he didn't know why Dan thought that he did. Jake's limitations were painfully obvious to him. However, he did not feel that he should be defined by those limitations and he saw no need in imposing limitations that did not truly exist.

Jake knew, from experience, that many obstacles that were caused by blindness could be overcome by ingenuity and determination. He felt that it was foolish to simply assume that a particular thing could not be done by a person just because that person was blind. Dan thought that this was a somewhat naive prospective, though Jake had proven it multiple times.

Jake knew that Dan thought that he was extraordinarily intelligent but he felt that Dan overestimated the limits that blindness imposed on his ability to use that intelligence. Jake and Dan had many conversations concerning this subject over the years but Dan never truly understood Jake's attitude. Eventually, long ago, they had come to an unspoken arrangement in which they agreed to disagree and they very rarely actually spoke directly of Jake's blindness or the things connected to it. Jake was disheartened by Dan's perception of him. Nevertheless, he loved is brother very much and was looking forward to trying to build a closer relationship with him.

Jake reached out and pressed the home button on his iPhone. The phone said "6:05". It was time to get up. He got up, brushed his teeth, showered, dressed, and headed down the hall to the kitchen, where he started the coffee.

While he waited for the coffee to brew, he went into his study and turned on his laptop. He had a new idea for a novel in his head and he wanted to create a rough outline of the plot. He would get started working on that in a few minutes, once he had his first cup of coffee beside him. For the moment, he would just get his computer up and going and check his E-mail.

In a minute or so, the musical tones sounded, indicating that the computer had booted up and was ready for use. A few seconds later, the computer said "JAWS for Windows is ready", indicating that his screen reading software was loaded and ready to go.

He opened Microsoft Outlook, which was his E-mail program of choice. He used the up and down arrows to move through the list of messages in his inbox. As he did so, JAWS read information concerning the sender of the message, the subject, and the time that the message had been received. There were a couple spam messages and then he came across a message that surprised him.

It was a message from Cathy, Dan's ex-wife. She and Jake had occasionally exchanged E-mails but they had not done so since she and Dan had divorced, six months ago, so he did not expect to have a message from her in his inbox. He pressed enter in order to open the message and he then pressed caps lock + down arrow, which was the JAWS command to read the area of the screen which had focus.

As he listened to JAWS read what Cathy had written, he became intrigued. Over the years, he had heard of many researchers who were working to cure blindness. However, most of them did not really hold out very much hope for him. For one thing, the causes of blindness were many and many of the techniques that had been explored by researchers would not work for his particular eye condition. In addition, most of the research that he had read about was decades away from producing any really meaningful results. He knew that Cathy knew these things as well because they had discussed it, more than once. So, if what she had read about this company and its research interested her, then perhaps it was worth him taking a look as well. He arrowed through the message until he came to the link to the company's website and he pressed enter to open the link.

The name of the company was "Vision Biotech" and, basically, the company was working to develop an electronic retina.

The retina is similar to the film or photo sensor in a camera. The retina is the thin layer of photosensitive tissue that lies at the back of the eye. Light passes through the cornea and lens, at the front of the eye, and these structures focus the light on the retina, which converts the patterns of light into nerve impulses that are then sent to the brain via the optic nerve.

If the retina does not function correctly then the individual will be visually impaired or, in Jake's case, completely blind. Jake had been born three months prematurely. When a baby is born that prematurely, the retina is not yet fully developed and, once the baby is outside of the mother, the remaining development of the retina, sometimes, does not occur normally. When this occurs, the condition is known as Retinopathy of Prematurity, ROP for short, and this was the condition which was responsible for Jake's blindness.

If a viable electronic retina were to be developed, then it could perform the function that Jake's damaged retinas could not and, thus, give him sight. The development of an artificial retina was not a new concept. Other researchers working for other biotech companies and universities had tried to develop artificial retinas previously and, though their efforts had met with some success, there had been problems that kept all of the previous efforts from really being a viable option.

Jake found the information on Vision Biotech's website fascinating. The company acknowledged that it was not the first to come up with the concept of an electronic artificial retina. It outlined the major successes by it's predecessors in the field and it explained the reasons why the earlier technology that had been developed was, as yet, not really a viable option. Jake already knew all of this. The website then explained that what was being done by the researchers of Vision Biotech was different and superior. It was this that grabbed Jake's attention.

The image sensors that had been used in previous attempts had a very low resolution, considerably less than one megapixel. In addition, these sensors had been monochromatic. The image sensor that Vision Biotech was using had a resolution of ten megapixels with a forty bit color depth. This was the first way in which the Vision Biotech approach was different from previous attempts and this difference, alone, was astounding.

The second way that the Vision Biotech method differed from previous attempts was in the way in which information was delivered to the brain. Previously, tiny electrodes corresponding to individual pixels had been implanted in the sub retinal space, where they were intended to stimulate the existing neural network of the eye to transmit these pixels to the brain. Other methods had involved implanting electrodes directly into the brain. Both of these methods were very limited in the number of pixels that could be represented. Also, the state of each pixel was binary, which meant that each pixel was simply either on or off and, therefore, it was not possible to transmit color in this way. Because of these limitations, even if better sensors had been previously used, it would not have been possible to transmit the resulting vast amount of complex data to the brain in a meaningful way that would have allowed for vision. Vision Biotech claimed to have overcome this limitation, though the website was very vague as to how this had been accomplished.

After Jake read through the information on the website, he sat back, stunned. His mind was flying through the possibilities. Ten megapixel vision, in color? Was it possible? If he had vision like that, he could even drive a car. Not only that, he could do absolutely anything that people with normal eyesight could do. Even ten megapixels did not represent the same vision that someone with normal, undamaged eyes had. Still, it would be close enough to allow him to do everything that they did.

Of course, he knew that just because the website said that this was close to becoming reality, that did not mean that it was so. Many companies had grandstanded, touting all kinds of unrealistic claims that never came to pass. However, none had touted claims like this. Could it really be?

As Cathy had said, the company was based in Memphis, which was just seventy or eighty miles down Interstate 40. Perhaps he should call them and find out if they would see him. If they were close to clinical trials, maybe they would consider him as a candidate. The website had a phone number but it was only 6:45 so, of course, there would not yet be anyone available. He copied the phone number and pasted it into the body of an E-mail to himself so that he could call later.

The coffee had finished brewing a while ago. Jake loved coffee and he always really looked forward to his first cup of the day. However, he had become engrossed in his reading on the Vision Biotech website so much that he hadn't even noticed the aroma of fresh coffee drifting through the house. He got up and, trailing the fingers of his right hand lightly along the wall, he hurried down the hall to get his first cup.

Back in the study, he sipped the coffee and thought about what he had read. His mind was still reeling. He was skeptical by nature and he hoped that he wasn't getting his hopes up for nothing but he couldn't shake the feeling that this might really be it. This could really mean a cure for his blindness, which was something that he had always assumed was impossible.

As he continued to sip his coffee, he went online and searched for articles about Vision Biotech. He found several, most of which just gave the exact same information that had been on the company's website. In most cases, it appeared that select portions had simply been copied and pasted. However, he did find a few articles in peer reviewed publications, such as the New England Journal of Medicine and Ophthalmology Today. He didn't understand all of the medical jargon in these articles but he did understand enough to know that, over all, the impressions in the medical community concerning this emerging technology were positive.

He checked the time. It was 8:06. He didn't know when people started arriving at Vision Biotech but he hoped that they were there by now. He couldn't wait any longer and so he was about to find out.

He picked up his iPhone and opened the E-mail message that he had previously sent to himself, which contained the phone number of the company's office. He double tapped on the number and the phone placed the call. It rang several times and he was just about to double tap the end button when a very pleasant female voice said "Vision Biotech, this is Christine, how may I help you".

"I'm glad that you picked up, I was about to give up and call later. I wasn't sure when you open."

"Oh, I'm sorry. We start at 8:00 but I have had a very hectic morning and I got here right as your call came through."

"No problem. I was just looking at your website and I was fascinated by what I read. I live in Jackson and I was wondering if I could make an appointment to come in and talk to someone."

"I can certainly transfer you to someone who can talk to you about that. First, may I ask, are you someone who could potentially benefit from our technology or a family member of such a person?"

"I, myself, am such a person. I have ROP."

"And your name?"

"Oh yes, I'm sorry, my name is Jake Richardson."

"OK Jake, hold on a second."

Jake thought that Christine must have one of the most pleasant and joyful voices that he had ever heard and that was saying a lot coming from a man who used his hearing as his primary sense and paid attention to voices like sighted people paid attention to faces and body language.

In just a few seconds, a man's voice came on the line.

"Mr. Richardson, this is Dr. Ben Nelson. What can I do for you?"

"Yes sir, I have ROP. I was just looking at your website and I was astounded by the information concerning the technology that you are working on. I was wondering if it might be possible to make an appointment to come in and talk to you about it."

"Certainly that is possible. When did you have in mind? At the moment, our schedule is wide open, though we suspect that will change once we take the next step."

Jake paused. He hadn't thought about timing of the appointment. Of course, he couldn't drive himself and he hadn't checked with his parents or Dan to see when they might be free to drive him down to Memphis. Perhaps he could get Dan to take him. He had wanted to spend time with Dan anyway and a little trip to Memphis could be fun for the two of them. After thinking for a moment, Jake spoke.

"Well, this is a little embarrassing. I was so excited about what I read on the website that I just called without first checking with someone to see when they might be able to drive me down there."

"That's quite alright. As I said, for the moment, our schedule is wide open. Would you like to make arrangements for transportation and call me back?"

"Yes. Thank you. I think that I will check and see if my brother can bring me down there. He has a lot of time on his hands just now so I'm sure that it won't be a problem. I will try to call you back sometime today."

Dr. Nelson's voice seemed to brighten.

"Excellent, excellent. I will look forward to receiving your call. Thank you, Mr. Richardson, for your interest in our technology."

"Thank you Dr. Nelson. Have a great day."

"Same to you sir."

Jake hung up. He was as excited as he could ever remember being. He couldn't wait to talk to Dan.

Chapter 7

Christine Dunning sat behind her desk and looked out at the currently empty reception area of Vision Biotech. She had just transferred Jake's call to Dr. Nelson. She wanted to just sit for a few minutes and collect herself. She had had a very hectic morning and was a bit frazzled.

The morning had started on the wrong note, first thing, when she had overslept. The previous day, which was a Monday, she had been off work. She was an amateur seamstress and had spent the weekend making several shirts and skirts for herself, from a few patterns that she had recently found. She made all of her own clothes. Sewing was very relaxing to her. It had a practical side as well because she was able to save a lot of money, which was important, because she didn't make all that much money. On Sunday evening, she was very pleased, having accomplished so much, but she was worn out. She planned to sleep in and relax on Monday and so she had turned off the wake up alarm on her iPhone and had then forgotten to turn it back on.

Instead of her usual wake up time of 6:00, her eyes had popped open promptly at 7:02. She jumped up and ran for the bathroom, where she showered in record time. Upon stepping from the shower, she found that there was no towel on the towel bar beside the shower. She had to walk across her apartment, naked and dripping wet, to retrieve a towel from the dryer. There was no time to iron any clothes so she grabbed a pair of slacks and one of the shirts that she had made over the weekend and quickly jumped into them.

She dashed into the kitchen. There was no time to make coffee or any kind of hot breakfast. She poured the last of the cereal, which was very little, into a bowl. When she grabbed the gallon of milk, which was nearly full, it slipped from her hand and busted when it hit the floor, splashing her with milk and drenching the entire kitchen floor. OK, forget breakfast. She got the remainder of the towels from the dryer and cleaned up the mess.

She dashed back to the bedroom to get out of her milk soaked clothes and find something else to wear. Her clothes were so thoroughly soaked through that even her bra and panties were wet. She found that there were none in her dresser. Another naked dash across the apartment to get some from the laundry basket on top of the washing machine. Thank goodness she had done laundry last night. Now, back to the bedroom where she found another pair of slacks and another of the shirts that she had recently made. She jumped into them even more quickly than she had done before.

Then, just as she was about to run out the door, before anything else could go wrong, her cell phone rang. She looked at the screen. It said "Roger Dunning". Crap!

She had met Roger ten years ago, when she was twenty. They had both been students at the University of Tennessee at Martin, both business majors. Roger's father owned West Tennessee Construction, a large construction company which was based in Memphis but which built commercial buildings all over the state. As he grew up, Roger had worked in every facet of the business, learning the ropes. His father was getting old and burned out. The plan was for Roger to take over the business after he had graduated college. She had liked that, unlike so many guys that she knew, he knew exactly what he wanted to do and had a plan for the future.

She also thought that he was very good looking. He was about 6'2" and weighed about 250 pounds, most of it muscle because he had spent most of his teenage years doing manual labor. He had a dark complexion, sandy blond hair, and green eyes. He turned a lot of heads as he walked across the campus of UTM.

He had more going for him than just his looks. During their courtship, he had been very attentive. He always called to check on her if she wasn't feeling well. He brought her flowers and little gifts, even if there was no special occasion. He always wanted to hear all about her interests and what was going on in her life. He did not pressure her about sex, as most other guys that she had dated did. All in all, he seemed to be the perfect gentleman.

After dating for three years, they were married. Shortly after the marriage, she began to see a side of Roger that he had not displayed during their courtship. He still had periods of time in which he was loving and attentive but there also began to be periods in which he was angry, shouting baseless accusations. She began to think that he might have a psychological disorder. Though she begged him to, he would not seek treatment. Living with him became hell on earth but she hung on for as long as she could. He did take over his father's company and he was gone a lot, overseeing construction projects. His frequent absences helped her to deal with the early years. The periods of anger became more and more frequent and longer lasting. Eventually, his angry outbursts escalated from shouting to violence. She couldn't stay with someone who she feared. Shortly after the violence began, she left him.

Christine had always hated divorce, because she knew that God hated it, and she felt guilty about her decision to leave Roger, even after all he had put her through. Still, she didn't know what else she could have done and she didn't believe that God would have her stay in a situation where she had good reason to fear for her safety.

Now, three years later, he still called occasionally, either in a rage or begging her to take him back. She didn't have time to deal with him this morning. She touched the decline button on her iPhone. More and more, this had become the way that she dealt with his calls. She hoped that, eventually, he would give up and stop calling. Of course, she knew that it could also make him even angrier but she didn't know what else to do.

As she dashed out of her bedroom, she briefly paused to examine herself in the full length mirror that was hung on the bedroom door. She was very slender, at about 5'2" and 110 pounds. She had lustrous, long, thick, blond hair that came about half way down her back. She usually wore it strait, which was a good thing because she didn't have time to do anything but run a brush through it this morning. She had a fair complexion and blue eyes that were very clear and sharp. She had been often told that she was very beautiful but she didn't see it. Right now though, all things considered, she thought that she looked good enough.

When she finally got to work, the phone was ringing when she walked in and she had to run to get it before the caller hung up. Now that she had handled the simple task of transferring the call, for the first time all morning, she could sit for a minute and do nothing but breathe.

She had had a harrowing morning but she was glad to be here. She enjoyed her work very much. She may have been just a secretary, greeting people, answering the phone, typing, filing, and such but, still, she was part of a company that was on the cutting edge of medicine and, with the work that this company was doing, it had the potential to make a real difference in thousands of lives. A cure for blindness. What could be more important? Perhaps a cure for cancer or diabetes but not much else. As mundane as her work might be, it contributed to what the company was doing and it made her feel good to be a part of it.

As she sat there, she looked down and saw a post-it note in the center of her desk blotter. It was a note from Dr. Nelson. It read "If Jake Richardson calls, get me, no matter where I am or what I am doing". The call that she had just taken was from Jake Richardson. It was a good thing that she hadn't been any later. She didn't know why Jake Richardson was so important but missing his call would certainly not have been a way to improve the morning that she was having.

Having missed breakfast, she was getting hungry and her stomach was beginning to growl. She decided to go back to the break room to get some coffee and see if there was anything to eat. She hummed as she walked down the hall. She had never been one to let a bad morning get her down. Sure enough, in the break room, in the middle of the table, there was an unopened box of doughnuts. However, the coffee pot was empty. She got out a filter and scooped in the coffee, inhaling deeply as she did so (she loved the smell of coffee). She put the filter in the brew funnel, put the brew funnel in the coffee maker, and pressed the brew button.

While she waited for the coffee to brew, she took a napkin from a dispenser, took a doughnut from the box, sat down at the table, and began to eat.

As she ate, she thought about the call from Roger. It troubled her. He had begun calling more often. At first, it had been about once per month, then twice per month, and now, twice last week. Sending his calls to voicemail and then not calling him back might be angering him and making him escalate his efforts. That scared her but she couldn't just let him bulldoze over her.

She wondered if she should again start carrying the gun that she had bought back when she first had become afraid of him. If she hadn't had it, she probably wouldn't have gotten away from him on that last day. She didn't like the idea of carrying it again but she liked the thought of getting her head bashed in even less.

She wondered when she would be able to get past what he had done to her. They had divorced three years ago and she hadn't even dated since. She wasn't down on men in general but she couldn't shake the feeling that if she got into another relationship, even if he seemed to be great, like Roger did at first, they would turn out to be heck on earth, just like Roger did. She knew that there had to be good men out there and that this was not a rational fear but, still, she couldn't help feeling this way.

The coffee finished brewing. She got a cup and another doughnut and headed back to her desk.

Once there, she turned on her computer and checked her E-mail. There was a message from Dr. Nelson.

Christine,

Jake Richardson should call back sometime today. If he does, give the call to me. If you can't get me for some reason, ask when it would be convenient for him to come in and make an appointment for me to meet with him. It doesn't matter when. If there is a conflict on my calendar, I will work around it.

Thanks,

Dr. Nelson

Strange. She had never seen Dr. Nelson give such priority to meeting with anyone. When she had taken his call, Jake had told her that he was interested in finding out more about the technology that Vision Biotech was developing because it might be able to help him. She took dozens of calls every week from people wanting to find out more about the technology and if it might be able to help them. Yet she had never seen Dr. Nelson give any of them this much attention. She wondered what it was that set Jake apart from the rest. Oh well, none of her business, she supposed.

She acknowledged the message and began to get her desk organized to start the day's work.

Chapter 8

Dan slowly began to drift toward consciousness. Eventually, the connections were made between the proper neurons in his brain that allowed him to realize that his phone was ringing. He reached out beside the bed and felt for his phone but he felt nothing but air. He remembered that this bed had no night stand beside it and so he had put his phone on the floor. Darn, he was going to have to stand up. He slowly and groggily got to his feet and bent down to retrieve the phone. By the time that he had accomplished this, the phone had stopped ringing. He looked at the screen to see who had been calling. It was Jake. Dan still felt a bit too groggy to carry on a conversation so, instead of calling him back, he replied via text.

"Hey bro. Long day yesterday and just woke up. Too tired to talk. Call you shortly."

He knew that Jake also had an iPhone and, as he touched the send button, he thought about how cool it was that he could send a text to a blind man and that blind man could read the message and reply, using only a touch screen. No sooner had he finished this thought than the phone vibrated in his hand.

"Hey yourself bro. Get your lazy butt up, slug down some coffee, and call me."

Dan smiled as he headed for the bathroom. He brushed his teeth, showered, shaved, and dressed. By the time that he was done, he smelled the odors of fresh coffee and frying bacon wafting up the stairs.

When he arrived in the kitchen, his mother said "well, glad you could finally join us".

He laughed.

Hey, it's my first day home. Can't you cut me some slack?

The voice of his father boomed "nope, we don't cut slack around here". Dan looked in the direction from which his father's voice had come and he saw his father coming down the hall to the kitchen from the study. His father added "we especially don't cut any slack for those who hold up breakfast". Gary clapped Dan on the back and, laughing, said "how did you sleep son".

"I slept like a log. Can't you tell by my holding up breakfast?"

Now Ramona cut in,"hush both of you and sit down at the table".

"yes mam", they both said in unison.

They all sat down to bacon, eggs, biscuits, and coffee.

Dan said "hey, now I could get use to this".

Gary said "yeah, I could too".

Ramona punched Gary on the arm.

Gary said "hey, I'm just saying".

As they ate, they talked. Dan caught up on the latest Jackson gossip from his mother and the goings on in the local business community from his father. After an hour, they had each eaten a plate full of food and, between them, they had drank a pot of coffee. Finally, Dan pushed back from the table.

"I missed a call from Jake earlier. Instead of calling him back, I think I'll just go on over there."

Ramona said "I wonder how he's coming on the book that he's writing".

Contemptuously, Gary said "the boy can't make a living writing, that's just a bunch of nonsense".

Ramona said "well Gary, everybody can't be a lawyer or accountant".

Dan said "well, he's got to do something and, who knows, it might work out". As he got up, he added "I'll see how he's doing with it in a few minutes, when I get over there". He then grabbed his keys and headed out the door.

As he made the short drive to Jake's house, Dan thought about what his father had said. He had to admit that his dad was probably right, it was unlikely that Jake could make a living writing. Then again, lots of people did make lots of money doing it and you didn't have to be a bestselling author to just make a living. Jake was probably the most intelligent person whom Dan had ever met. If only he could see, he would have any number of careers from which to choose. Dan thought "if only I could, somehow, make that happen".

Jake lived in a small and quiet subdivision that had been developed in the 1950s and 1960s. His house was a three bedroom, two bathroom, with about 1,800 square feet. Dan had purchased the house for Jake about five years previous and he paid for someone to keep up the yard. He felt that was the least that he could do, given his wealth and the uphill climb that Jake faced. When Dan pulled into the driveway, he just sat there, looking at the house for a few minutes, still thinking about Jake and his limited career choices. Dan thought "if only I could change it, if only I could make it easier for him, I would give everything that I have to make that happen".

Suddenly, the front door flew open. Jake stood there, looking toward the spot where Dan's truck sat, though he could not have known where it was. He called out "well, Dan, are you going to sit there all day". Dan smiled. He had missed his brother.

Dan got out and went to the front door. He pumped Jake's hand vigorously and then embraced him. When they disengaged, Dan spoke.

"Just now, when you came to the door, when I was still sitting in my truck, you looked straight at me. How did you know that it was me and how did you know where to look? It amazes the heck out of me how you do things like that."

Jake laughed.

"Well, first of all, it had to be you because you and Dad are the only people who I know that drive trucks that sound like Godzilla is eating them and then throwing them back up, so it had to be one of you, and your truck idles a little faster than Dad's does. As far as how I knew where to look, I have a driveway, not a parking lot, and I assumed that you didn't park on the roof so there was pretty much only one choice as to where you could be."

Dan cracked up. He had always loved Jake's sense of humor.

Jake said "well, come on in and sit down".

The front part of the house was rectangular. You stepped through the front door into a narrow entry hall with a solid wall to the left and a half wall with spindles up to the ceiling on the right. On the other side of this half wall was a small dining room. If you proceeded to the end of the entry hall, to the left was a hall that led to the bedrooms and bathrooms. To the right was a large open area which was comprised of the kitchen, which was very small, and eat in area, which contained a small table with four chairs. At the back of this open area was about a six inch step down into an area that had been added onto the house at some point, prior to Jake's living here. This addition contained a den, which was long and rectangular, about 24 by 12. At one end of the den was a door that led into a large laundry room. On the back wall of the den was a large brick fireplace which was flanked on both sides by built in book shelves.

Having just stepped from the entry hall, Dan could see the entire main living area of the house and he could see that everything was in perfect order. The floor was clean and appeared to have been recently vacuumed. Knickknacks were lined up on the mantel of the fireplace in an arrangement that was pleasing to the eye. On the bookshelves sat books and pictures that were mostly aligned and angled correctly. A few things sat a skew because, if something got knocked out of place, Jake didn't notice, unless he felt of it, and he didn't go around feeling of everything all of the time. It amazed Dan that everything was mostly in order. Heck, he knew people who could see who didn't keep house this well.

Dan followed Jake into the den. At one end of the rectangular room sat two sofas, perpendicular to each other. Dan sat on one and Jake sat on the other.

"So, Jake, how have you been?"

"I'm doing very well."

"I like your place here. Looks like you're taking good care of it."

"Of course I am."

"Are you still planning on trying to make a career as a writer?"

"Sure am."

"How is that going?"

"I finished the first novel. It's relatively short and I'm not sure that it's worth trying to publish but I learned a lot in the process of writing it. I have an idea for another novel. This morning, I have been working on outlining the plot, although I have been having problems concentrating."

"Problems concentrating? Writers block?"

"No, nothing like that. I have my mind on something else and I can't wait to tell you about it."

"Really? Tell me."

"Well, strangely enough, it started with an E-mail from Cathy."

"Cathy? My ex-wife?"

"One and the same. I found it a bit strange too because I haven't heard anything from her since you guys split up."

"Well, what did she say?"

"She had run across the website of a biotech company that is pursuing a cure for blindness. They are working on an electronic artificial retina."

"Haven't there been others who have done that and haven't they all had problems?"

"Yes, they all have either had problems or simply not been practical but it looks like this one might be different. At least, I hope it is."

Jake summarized for Dan what he had read on the website of Vision Biotech and what he had found in his subsequent online research. Dan was impressed.

"You say that this company is in Memphis?"

"Yes."

"Well, maybe we need to go down there."

"That's what I thought and I had hoped that you would see it my way. I have already called and they have agreed to see me but I didn't set up an appointment yet. I wanted to talk to you first to see if you would be willing to go down there with me."

"Sure, I'd love to. Sounds fun. I have plenty of time on my hands at the moment. Call and make the appointment, doesn't matter when."

"Do you want me to call now?"

"Yeah, sure. Why wait?"

Jake placed the call and Christine again transferred him to Dr. Nelson, who seemed very excited to hear from him. They set up an appointment for the following day at 10:00am.

The two brothers talked for a while longer and then Dan excused himself, saying that he had a few things to take care of. Jake indicated that he understood and that, in fact, he needed to work on his writing for a while, especially given that he wouldn't be able to write any the next day because of the appointment at Vision Biotech. The brothers again embraced and Dan left.

Dan grabbed a burger and fries at McDonalds and ate in the parking lot. Afterword, he drove around south Jackson. It had been a long time since he had been here and he wanted to see what had changed and reminisce about what hadn't changed. Also, it wouldn't hurt to keep an eye out for a house and some suitable office space.

As he drove, he thought about what Jake had told him about Vision Biotech. It seemed almost too good to be true. Even if the claims on the website weren't exaggerated, they could be years from clinical trials and, even when they got to that stage, if they got to that stage, it could be years more before the technology became available to the public. He hadn't mentioned any of this to Jake. For one thing, he knew that Jake was certainly intelligent enough to have thought of these things for himself. Also, Jake was so excited and Dan just hated to do anything that might bring him down. Dan thought "I guess tomorrow, we shall see".

Chapter 9

Ben Nelson sat back in his office chair. He was very pleased. The first piece of the puzzle was falling into place quite nicely. He had just spoken to Jake Richardson. He was coming tomorrow and, more importantly, his brother was coming with him. This darned plan might just work after all.

He could feel the brass ring within his grasp and it was about time. He had founded Vision Biotech five years ago and it had been a hard yet exhilarating five years.

Back then, he had only a concept of the technology that now underlay the work of the company. However, he had been able to convince enough people of the validity of his conceptual technology to allow him to obtain a one million dollar grant from the American Institute of Ophthalmological Research (AIOR). With this grant, he had started the company. Though he understood the technology that he was developing, he had little understanding of how much money that it would take to bring the technology from the conceptual stage to the operating room. That first million was gone within a year. He was able to obtain a second grant from AIOR and it was gone even faster. After much cajoling, he was even able to convince AIOR to come through with a third grant. As the research progressed, so did the capital burn rate. AIOR had said that there had not been sufficient progress to warrant a fourth grant and no amount of cajoling would convince them.

Ben was not about to let all of his hard work go down the drain without a fight. He started looking for venture capitalists. The potential financial rewards were virtually limitless but the risks were also quite high. After all, he wasn't the first to venture into this arena and, though some of his predecessors had some limited success which had laid the foundation for his work, none of them had had sufficient success to turn any real profit. Ben truly believed that the work that he was doing was different but he could not convince any investors of that.

Just when he had thought that all was lost, he was approached by Vinnie Patrillo. Mr. Patrillo had explained that he represented an organization that specialized in investing in high risk ventures and that, in return, his organization expected high returns, very high returns. He had further explained that his organization was prepared to invest a very large sum in Vision Biotech, provided that they could agree on acceptable terms.

Mr. Patrillo had been very ambiguous about the exact nature of the organization which he represented. Ben had always suspected that the organization was involved with, if not run by, organized crime. As long as Mr. Patrillo's organization could and would come up with the money that he needed, he didn't really care where the money came from.

They did, in fact, agree on acceptable terms and Mr. Patrillo's organization began pouring money into Vision Biotech. That had been two years ago and Mr. Patrillo was beginning to get impatient. He thought that, by now, his organization should have started to see some return on their investment or, at the very least, a slow down on the cash burn rate.

Perhaps it was an understatement to say that Vinnie was becoming impatient. He had been impatient six months ago. Now, he was downright ticked. Not much made Ben nervous but Vinnie Patrillo made him very nervous. He had a feeling that Vinnie was used to getting his way and he had a feeling that, when he didn't, he could become very unpleasant.

As though his thoughts of Vinnie had prompted it, the speaker on his phone came to life and Christine said "Dr. Nelson, there is a Mr. Patrillo for you on line two". Crap! He said "OK Christine, thanks, I'll get it in a minute".

Ben sat for several seconds and composed himself. He was sure that Vinnie was again going to harass him about the fact that Vinnie's organization had, as yet, not seen any return on their ongoing investment and he thought that Vinnie might step up the pressure to produce some returns. He didn't want to think about what stepping up the pressure might mean for a guy like Vinnie. At least things weren't as bleak as they might be. He did have the plan, involving Dan and Jake, which was off to a good start. He could explain to Vinnie that he was doing something that should get some money coming in soon. Emboldened by this thought, he picked up the phone.

"Hello Mr. Patrillo."

"Now Ben, I have told you, no need to be so formal, call me Vinnie."

"OK Vinnie."

"So, Ben, how are things going in Memphis this fine morning?"

"Things are going very well. How are things going in Chicago?"

"Things are just great here, just great. Thanks for asking."

"So, Vinnie, what can I do for you?"

"Well, an associate and I were just going over our financial records that relate to Vision Biotech. We would like for you to verify some information for us. We want to make sure that what is in your records matches what is in ours. Could you take a few minutes to help us out with that?"

"Oh yes, sure."

A little of Ben' new confidence left him. He knew what was coming.

"Ben, how long have we been doing business?"

"A little over two years."

"Yes, twenty-seven months, to be exact. Twenty-seven months ago, what was the amount of our initial investment in Vision Biotech?"

"It was one and a half million."

"Yes, that is what our records show. And then, one year later, fifteen months ago, what was the amount of our second investment?"

"That second investment was two and a half million."

"Yes, that is what our records show as well. As I recall, it took some convincing on your part to talk us into such a large investment the second time around but we came through, did we not?"

Ben tried to swallow a lump that was beginning to form in his throat.

"Yes sir, you did come through, and that was quite generous of you and your organization."

"Generous? Oh no, it wasn't generous. If the money was a gift, then that would have been generous. However, it wasn't a gift. We expected to get the money back, plus a large return. Now then, how much are we up to so far?"

"With the first and second investments, that would total four million."

Vinnie whistled.

84

"Man, four million. Is it that much? Yes, I suppose that would be about right. That isn't all though. Do you remember when we first started doing business and you were complaining about that dump that you were using for your lab and office space?"

"Yes, I remember."

"And, after about three months of your complaining, we helped you to find the space that you now occupy, didn't we?"

"Yes sir, you did."

"We arranged for you to occupy that space without a charge from the landlord. Do you recall what the rent on that space was, before we intervened on your behalf?"

"I believe that it was ten thousand per month."

"Yes, ten thousand per month. After twenty-four months, that would come to 240 thousand. I think we will just round that up to an even quarter million. That OK with you Ben?"

"Yes sir, that's just fine with me."

"OK, now, it looks like the total amount of our investment, to date, is about 4.25 million. That sound about right to you?"

"Yes sir, it does."

"And do you recall what the agreement was regarding repayment and return on our investment?"

"Yes sir. The agreement was that you would receive twice the amount of your investment back within eighteen months."

"Yes, twice the investment back within eighteen months. It has now been twenty-seven months. How much money have we gotten back from Vision Biotech?"

85

"None."

"What was that? You were mumbling a bit there."

"I said none. You have not received any money."

"Absolutely correct! None! Zero! Zilch! Now, Ben, why is that?"

Ben had to swallow a couple of times in order to get rid of the lump in his throat, which had gotten much bigger.

"Well, sir, as I have told you, we had some unforeseen delays in the final stages of our research and development."

"Delays? You said nothing about potential delays when we chose to invest with you."

"I did not foresee the potential for delays. Work like this is very complex and there is always the chance for things not to go exactly as planned. I do have some good news though."

"Good news? I could use some good news. Tell me."

"We are almost ready to begin clinical trials. We have identified a patient who would be perfect for our first clinical trial. Of course, with the clinical trial phase comes additional expenses."

"Additional expenses! You had better not be about to ask me for more money after the discussion that we have just been having!"

"No, Mr. Patrillo, not at all. This patient has a very wealthy brother. We think that we can get him to invest the money that will be necessary to get the first clinical trial out of the way. Once we have proven that the technology really can do what we have been saying that it can, we will be in a position to take the company public. The initial public offering for the company which has developed the cure for blindness will be huge. At that point, we will have no problem at all paying you every penny that we owe you."

There was silence for several seconds. Then, Vinnie spoke, in a calmer voice.

"And how long do you think that we are talking about here."

"Six months. Just give me six months. If you will do that, I can triple your money. In fact, we will just round it up to fifteen million. How does that sound?"

There was Silence for several more seconds. Then, Vinnie spoke quietly.

"OK, it's a deal. I will give you six months. At the end of that six months, you will have my fifteen million or I will have something for you that you will not like but you won't have long to not like it. Do we understand each other?"

Ben' mouth went dry and his bowels turned liquid. He really thought that he might be about to crap in his pants right there. When he finely managed to speak, it was in a strained voice.

"Yes sir, Mr. Patrillo. We understand each other perfectly."

"Good, very good. Good bye, Ben. Have a good day and a productive six months."

After Vinnie hung up, Ben dashed for the bathroom. He barely made it in time to vomit up what felt like everything that he had eaten in the last week. No sooner had he retched up the last mouth full of spittle than his bowels began to cramp. He barely had time to stand, turn around, drop his pants, and sit down, before what felt like all of his guts fell out.

As he sat there, he thought about the fact that he had not understood what he had gotten into with Vinnie and his organization. Sure, he had thought that Vinnie might be involved with organized crime, in fact he was quite sure of it, but he hadn't thought that the stakes would ever come down to this. He had been so wrapped up in the windfall that he was sure was coming. He hadn't really thought about what might happen with a guy like Vinnie, if things didn't go according to plan. Vinnie had just clarified things. Clearly, either Ben came up with the money in six months or he was dead. This plan involving Dan and Jake just had to work. No matter what, it had to work.

Chapter 10

Steve Levet walked into the presidential suite of the Sheraton Hotel, located on Waikiki Beach, on the Hawaiian island of Honolulu. He put down his two carry-on bags on one of the king size beds and quickly surveyed the suite. It had two bedrooms and a large living room. He thought that it would serve his purpose. He went out onto the balcony and took in the stunning view of Waikiki beach and the Pacific Ocean while he gathered his thoughts. About an hour before, he had arrived at Honolulu International Airport. He had quickly grabbed his luggage and hurried to the hotel. Although he was staying at one of the nicest hotels on Honolulu, in the most luxurious suite, he was not here for pleasure.

Steve was the manager of what was referred to simply as "The Fund". Each of the five largest health insurance companies in the United States annually contributed five million dollars to the fund, giving the fund a total influx of twenty-five million dollars per year. This was a very small amount in comparison to the overall revenue and expenses of these companies, a small enough amount that it could be funneled out of the companies, under the nose of accountants and regulators, without being noticed by anyone. The money was covertly used for various purposes, most of them illegal, in order to increase the profitability of the insurance industry. All of this was done under the direction of Steve, who drew a five million dollar salary from the fund. None of the fund's contributors said anything about this because Steve got things done that no one else could get done and, in so doing, he made them much more money than he cost them.

Two weeks previously, Steve had called a meeting of the fund's contributors in order to discuss how to handle a potential threat to the industry that was looming on the horizon. That threat was a little biotech company that, if successful in its attempt to develop a cure for blindness, had the potential to cause a very big monetary headache for the health insurance industry. It was starting to look like this little company was getting very close to proving the technology that it had been working on. Something had to be done about that and that was why this meeting had been called, which was scheduled to convene in about an hour.

In this case, doing something about the problem was going to mean someone getting hurt. They might even die. That didn't bother Steve in the least. He did what had to be done in order to insure the maximum profitability of his clients and, if something got in his way, he just ran over or through it. If that something happened to be a human life, so be it. His work didn't often involve killing but, when it did, he lost no sleep over it. To him, that was just business.

He walked back into the suite and began to prepare for the meeting that he was about to conduct. The suite had two bed rooms, one on either side of a large living room. He decided that he would use one of the bedrooms for an office and he would use the living room for a conference room. The bedroom that he chose for his office had a large dresser on one wall and a medium sized desk in one corner. He sat his computer bag on the dresser and began to remove its contents. There was a laptop computer, a compact printer/scanner, paper and ink for the printer, a surge protector, an extension cord, and various other cables and supplies. He setup the laptop computer and printer on the desk. His only other piece of luggage was a briefcase and he placed it on the bed. He unpacked his files and placed them on the bed as well. He had a change of clothes and a small shaving kit in a side pouch of the computer bag. Other than that, everything that he had brought was related to the task at hand. He would be staying only one night and his only purpose for being here was to conduct this meeting. As always, he was all business.

He sat down at the desk and got to work. He looked over the information that he would need for the meeting, though he had memorized all of it already. He printed a single page handout that he had prepared for each of the attendees. From the bed, he gathered a few files which contained some additional supporting information that he might need. He then went into the living room, placed the paperwork on the coffee table, sat down, and waited.

At precisely 3:00pm, there was a knock at the door. When Steve answered the knock, he found all five health insurance company CEOs standing there. All of them knew that he was a stickler for punctuality and they had arrived virtually simultaneously at the appointed time. Though they technically employed him, at these meetings, and in all matters involving the fund, he was in charge and they knew it. Steve would have it no other way. With all of the money that he made them, they couldn't afford to lose him so they put up with it. This arrangement was understood by all on both sides.

Steve said "the recliner is mine and the rest of you sit where ever you like". Besides the recliner, there were two sofas, which were arranged in an L configuration with the round coffee table in front of them. Steve had moved the recliner so that it sat directly across the coffee table from the juncture of the two couches. He sat down and looked slightly to his left and right, surveying the other men in the room. He met each man's gaze, in turn, and then he spoke.

"Well, you all know basically why we are here."

All of the others nodded in unison.

"OK, well, here it is in a nut shell. Vision Biotech has been working on a way to cure blindness. They have been working on an electronic artificial retina and a new way to interface that retina with the brain. The artificial retina is revolutionary in itself but the thing that is extraordinary is the interface. It can communicate images to the brain with extremely high resolution and it actually bypasses much of the optic nerve so it has the potential to even help people who have vision problems that are caused by damage to the optic nerve, like glaucoma. There are about 1.3 million legally blind people in the United States. About 25% of those, or about 375 thousand, are

91

covered by private health insurance. It looks like this technology will be able to help about 60 to 65 percent of these people, so we're talking about 200 thousand or so. Of course, I don't yet know how much the procedure will cost, as it isn't being offered yet, but my sources tell me that we are probably talking about half a million or so, perhaps a bit more. So, you see, we could easily be looking at an expenditure of over 100 billion on the part of health insurance."

One of the CEOs spoke up.

"Well, Steve, what kind of time table are we looking at here."

"Good question. Though we think they are close, we don't know exactly how close they are. They are having some financial problems and that has slowed them down some. If they find a solution to those financial problems, most likely in the form of an investor, then I think that it may only be five or six months until they are ready for clinical trials. Of course, there is no way to know how long it will take to find an investor. I think that the investor that has been funding them has cut them off entirely and so their next investor is going to have to shell out some big bucks, probably at least a million."

"So, are there any potential investors out there?"

"None that are on my radar. However, in this case, that doesn't really mean much. They probably need one to two million to get to clinical trials. That is a lot of money and it isn't. I mean it isn't small change but, on the other hand, a lot of people do have a couple million. The potential returns are huge. This company is getting a lot of good press. At any time, someone who is chasing a dollar or someone who has a relative who could benefit from the technology might step forward to fund them. I doubt it will be very long, which is why I have called this meeting."

"OK, let's assume that you are right. Let's assume that an investor will pop up tomorrow and, six months after that, they will be ready for clinical trials, after which, they will be pretty much unstoppable. What can we do about it?"

"Now, you see, you just hit the nail on the head. If the clinical trials are successful then they will be able to attract virtually unlimited funding and they will be absolutely unstoppable. We have to influence the outcome of the clinical trials so that they never get to that point. We have to screw up the first clinical trial so badly that there won't be any more."

"And how do you propose to do that?"

"Do you really want to know?"

"No, probably not."

"OK, I'll tell you anyway. Vision Biotech is developing the technology but they will not actually manufacture the hardware. The interface will be manufactured by a company called Biotronics. I don't have any contacts there but, with enough money, you can make contacts anywhere. I plan to introduce a slight modification to the interface hardware that will be used in the first clinical trial. I admit that I don't yet know the exact nature of the modification. After all, this technology is a very closely guarded secret. I don't exactly have a schematic. I will have to make contact with the person at Biotronics who will make the modification and he or she can provide me with information on what type of modification may be possible. I will take that information and go from there."

"Do you anticipate any, uh, fatalities in the first clinical trial?"

"Well, I hope so or, at least, a severe injury. I want something that will get a whole lot of bad press and be very discouraging to prospective investors and prospective patients. I want to kill the project and I want it to stay dead. Given that this interface device connects, more or less, directly to the brain, I doubt that it will be all that difficult to bring about a very catastrophic outcome."

After the meeting broke up, Steve sat down at his computer. Now that the fund contributors had given the OK for a basic course of action, he wanted to develop a plan. He would start by finding a prospective contact at Biotronics. He had several electronic resources for finding out just about anything about someone, some of them legal, most of them not. He spent several hours probing into every corner of the lives of each of Biotech's employees. By the time that he shut down the computer and went to bed, he knew exactly what he was going to do.

Chapter 11

At 5:30pm, Christine stepped out of her Ford Explorer in the parking lot of her apartment complex. She was glad to be home from work. Although she had overslept that morning, she was very tired. She had started the day in a panicked rush and that always left her drained. Fortunately, her work day hadn't been bad. Dr. Nelson had stayed locked in his office for most of the morning. Then, Jake Richardson had called back and made an appointment to see him the next day and, after that, he had been in an unusually good mood, which made the day easier to bear. He was usually pleasant enough but he was a bit of a perfectionist and that could sometimes be a bit exacerbating. Thankfully, she hadn't had to deal with that today. So, though she was tired, she was in a good mood. As she walked across the parking lot from her car to her first floor apartment, she was thinking about ordering a pizza, watching a little TV, and going to bed.

As she approached her door, she had her keys in her hand and was about to insert the key in the lock when she felt a hand very firmly and painfully grip her left shoulder. She spun around and her heart rate doubled. Her voice came out in a high pitched squeal, "Roger!"

He was standing only inches away from her and, as he was a foot taller, she had to crane her neck to look up at him. His face was impassive and, as she looked into his green eyes, she could not read his emotional state. However, the way that he had gripped her shoulder, which was still hurting, suggested that he was very angry. She didn't know exactly what he had in mind but she knew that his appearance here could not be good. When she spoke again, her voice was more under control, though her emotions were not.

"Roger, you hurt me when you grabbed my shoulder. Please calm down."

When he spoke, his voice was mostly calm but had a hard edge to it.

"I hurt you? Well, you have been hurting me too. You have been ignoring my calls."

"Yes, I know. Your calls upset me. I have asked you to stop but you won't."

He appeared to not hear her.

"I called this morning. You didn't answer."

"Yes, I know. But, Roger, listen."

His voice was rising now.

"I called last Friday and you didn't answer."

"Yes, Roger, I know. Roger, please listen."

"I called last Tuesday too. You didn't answer then either."

"Roger, please."

He was yelling now.

"Please Roger! Please Roger! Please Roger! Please what! After all of those years together, you expect to just be able to shut me out of your life! You think that you can get away with not even talking to me! Well, you're wrong about that you little twit!"

"Is there a problem here?"

Both Christine and Roger turned to see a man about Roger's height, though of smaller build. He stood about 20 feet away and had a medium sized pistil held in his right hand. He was John Fletcher, Christine's neighbor. He was a supervisor for FedEx, which was based there in Memphis. He had just arrived home from work and couldn't help but notice the commotion as he approached his apartment. Now, he looked directly at Roger as he spoke.

"I said is there a problem. It doesn't look as though Ms. Christine is too happy to be talking to you."

Roger's voice was quieter than it had been but very hard when he spoke.

"Our conversation is none of your business jerk."

"Well, ordinarily, I would agree that Christine's conversations are none of my business but, if she is being forced to have the conversation, then I would say that is my business."

Roger looked at John appraisingly. Christine knew that he was sizing him up, deciding if he could take him. In a physical fight, he probably could. However, there was the gun. She hoped that Roger would fear the gun enough to make him back off. When Roger was in a rage like this, she knew that he didn't think rationally. She didn't want to see Roger get shot. If it came to that, she didn't even know if John could pull the trigger. If not, she didn't want to think about what might happen if Roger managed to take the gun away from him.

After a tense moment, Roger simply turned and left, without saying anything. Christine saw him get into his truck, which she hadn't noticed earlier, and drive away.

As he approached her, John spoke.

"I'm glad that's over. There for a minute, I wasn't sure how it was going to go. Are you OK?"

"Yes, I think so."

"Did he hurt you?"

"Not really. He hurt my shoulder when he grabbed it. It might be bruised but it's OK."

He offered the gun.

"Do you need this? As a route supervisor, I occasionally have to fill in for a driver who doesn't show up at the last minute. I got this gun and a permit to carry it because you never know what you may run into out there but I've never had to use it. I would be happy to let you borrow it, if you think that he may be back."

"No, that's sweet of you to offer but I have one. I got it shortly before Roger and I split up. I haven't carried it in a while but I think that I will start again."

"Yeah, I think that's a good idea. Do you need anything? Are you going to call the police? I would be happy to talk to them with you. I saw most of it."

"No, I'm not going to call the police. They wouldn't really do anything. Thank you for the offer though and thank you for saving me from Roger. I don't know what would have happened if you hadn't come along."

"No problem. If you need anything, I'm right next door and Nancy and I aren't going anywhere tonight so just call and we will be right here."

She said "thanks" as she turned and shakily inserted the key into the lock.

Once she was safely inside her apartment and had locked the door and put on the safety chain, she just stood there for a couple minutes, shaking. Then, she dashed for the bathroom, as fast as she could run. She hit the tile floor on her knees and slid the last few inches to the commode. She got there barely in time. She violently heaved up everything in her stomach and kept heaving for a minute after that. After she flushed, she shakily got to her feet and washed her face. As she stood there looking into the mirror, she pulled off her shirt and looked at her shoulder. There were finger shaped bruises. The sight of them brought on another wave of nausea but she held it down. She put her shirt back on and went into her bedroom.

She reached into her nightstand and pulled out her 38 caliber Smith and Wesson revolver. She swung out the cylinder and dumped out the five rounds into her hand. She closed the cylinder and cocked the gun. In the quiet room, the click click of the hammer drawing back sounded loud. She pulled the trigger and the snap sounded even louder. The weight of the gun felt good in her hand. She reloaded the gun and laid it on the bed. In the drawer, she found the registration for the gun and her concealed carry permit, both of which she folded and placed into her wallet. She intended to carry the gun and she might need the documents to prove that that it was legal for her to have and carry it. Though it was warm, she felt a bit chilled. She got a light jacket from the closet and put the gun in the pocket. It made her feel better to have it with her, even inside the apartment.

She no longer wanted pizza. She decided to make a sandwich, take a bath, and go to bed. She only hoped that she would be able to sleep.

Chapter 12

The next morning, Dan and Jake walked into Vision Biotech. The reception area was relatively small. On one wall, beside the door, was a sofa. Beside it was an end table with a lamp. Directly across from the sofa, a few feet away, was a desk, behind which sat a stunningly beautiful woman. She had dark circles under her eyes, as though she perhaps hadn't slept well but, still, Dan thought that she had to be one of the most beautiful women that he had ever seen. When he and Jake walked up to the desk, she said "I'm Christine, welcome to Vision Biotech". Jake told her that he had a 10:00am appointment to see Dr. Nelson. Though Christine looked tired, she was very pleasant. She said that she remembered making the appointment and she asked them to take a seat, adding that Dr. Nelson would be right with them.

Dan and Jake sat on the sofa. After Christine hung up the phone, having announced them to Dr. Nelson, she said that she remembered that they lived in Jackson and asked them if they had had a nice trip. No sooner had Dan replied that the trip had been very pleasant than Dr. Nelson appeared in the door behind Christine. Dan couldn't help but wish that he had had a bit more time to chat with her.

Dr. Nelson came around the desk and introduced himself, offering his hand. Jake, assuming that Dr. Nelson would be offering his hand, reached out his own hand and shook.

"Pleased to meet you Dr. Nelson, I'm Jake Richardson."

"Hi Jake. Please, call me Ben."

"Thank you Ben. This is my brother, Dan."

Ben shook Dan's hand and led them down the hall. As this was an unfamiliar environment, Jake took Dan's arm so that Dan

101

could lead him. Mostly for Jake's benefit, Ben explained their surroundings.

"OK, we are going through a door that is behind Ms. Christine here. Now, we are in a hall that is about four feet wide and perhaps 40 feet long. On the left side of the hall is a bathroom, a small break room, and an opthomological exam room. On the right side of the hall are three offices, belonging to myself, Dr. Fleming, and Dr. Crowder. At the opposite end of the hall is a door that leads into our lab space, which I will show you in a little while. Right now, let's go into my office, which is the first door on your right."

They went into the office, which was relatively small, perhaps 12 by 12 feet. It contained a paper strewn desk, behind which was a high backed leather chair, and, behind that, a credenza on which sat a laptop computer and a telephone. In front of the desk were two small side chairs. Ben explained the layout of the room to Jake and then invited them to take a seat. Dan guided Jake to a chair before sitting himself.

Ben Spoke.

"Jake, I believe that you said that you have ROP. Is that correct?"

"Yes sir, that is correct."

"What is your visual acuity?"

"My ROP is at stage 4+. I have no vision in either eye, only a little light perception, on a good day."

"Is ROP the only issue that exists with your eyes?"

"Yes, but that's enough, don't you think?"

They all laughed.

"Yes, it surely is enough. I just want to make sure that there are no other problems that might prevent you from being a candidate for this technology."

Jake's heart quickened.

"Candidate? You mean that this technology is already available?"

"Wait just a second. Let's not get ahead of ourselves. First of all, I'd like to explain the technology and then we can go from there. Sound OK?"

Jake and Dan both nodded.

"OK, if you have looked at our website, then you may already know some of this but bear with me. OK, first thing first. Let me explain the function of the retina. The retina is similar to the film or photo sensor in a camera. The retina is the thin layer of photosensitive tissue that lies at the back of the eye. Light passes through the cornea and lens, at the front of the eye, and these structures focus the light on the retina, which converts the patterns of light into nerve impulses that are then sent to the brain via the optic nerve. In your case, Jake, your retinas are damaged, due to your premature birth, and this is what is responsible for your blindness. You probably already knew that. Are you with me so far?"

Jake and Dan nodded.

"With current technology, it is not possible to restore function to retinas that are damaged as badly as yours are. It is also not possible to successfully transplant a retina. I'm sure that you already knew these things."

Jake and Dan nodded again.

"Given that these things are not possible, the only remaining solution would be for someone to come up with an artificial retina and find a way to interface that retina with the brain. This is what we have done. Now, as you may be aware, this approach has been attempted before and has met with only very limited success. However, what we have done is different, in two ways. First of all, the image sensors that were used in previous attempts had a very low resolution, considerably less than one megapixel. In addition, these sensors were monochromatic. The image sensor that we have developed has a resolution of 15 megapixels with a forty bit color depth."

Jake interrupted.

"Wait, the website said that the resolution of the sensor is ten megapixels."

"Oh yes, I'm sorry, that information is a little bit out of date. We have recently found a way to increase the resolution of the sensor. The second way our technology differs from previous attempts is in the way in which information is delivered to the brain. Previously, tiny electrodes corresponding to individual pixels had been implanted in the sub retinal space, where they were intended to stimulate the existing neural network of the eye to transmit these pixels to the brain. Other methods involved implanting electrodes directly into the brain. Both of these methods were very limited in the number of pixels that could be represented. Also, the state of each pixel was binary, which means that each pixel was simply either on or off and, therefore, it was not possible to transmit color in this way. Because of these limitations, even if better sensors had been previously used, it would not have been possible to transmit the resulting vast amount of complex data to the brain in a meaningful way that would have allowed for vision. We have overcome this limitation."

Much to the delight of Ben, Jake could not remain silent.

"How, how, how!"

Ben smiled broadly.

"Well, I'm glad you asked. We have developed an interface device, which is separate from the sensor device, which is capable of delivering very complex visual information to the brain in a way that the brain can interpret."

"Is this interface device implanted directly into the brain? I'm not sure that I would like that."

"No no no. It connects to the brain but it is not implanted in the brain. It connects to the optic nerve, just posterior to the fundic disk."

"But, the fundic disk is behind the retina."

"That is correct. I'm pleased to see that you understand the structure of the eye. It makes explaining things much easier. The retina is removed, as well as several layers of cells from the anterior portion of the optic nerve. The interface device resides and is connected there. The photo sensor is placed within the vitriol space. The framework that keeps the photo sensor stable and correctly oriented is attached to the wall of the posterior chamber, with the sensor itself extending slightly into the anterior chamber. The remaining vitriol space is then flooded with an inert fluid that has the approximate viscosity of natural vitriol humor. Did you understand all of that?"

"Yes."

Dan broke in.

"Well, I didn't understand but maybe every third word of that. I'm not even sure that it was English. Could one of you translate that?"

Jake turned to Dan.

"They take out the fluid in the eye as well as the retina. They attach a frame to the walls of the eye, near the back, which holds what amounts to a little camera, which sends a signal to a device at the very back of the eye, that translates and sends that signal to the brain through the optic nerve."

Laughing, Dan said "oh, OK, why didn't you say that in the first place. Also laughing, Jake said "he did".

Ben smiled again.

"Hey, I'm impressed. Perhaps I should hire you rather than simply considering you as a candidate for the first clinical trial."

Jake's jaw slowly dropped and a look of astonishment came over his face.

"Um, candidate for the first clinical trial? Um, are you serious?"

"Ben' grin spread until it appeared that his nose might fall into his mouth."

"Sure, why not? We are close to being ready. The cause of your blindness is a retinal condition that is well suited for this procedure. Plus, I'm just impressed with you. I have a feeling that you could go very far with close to perfect vision. By the way, the interface device is capable of processing up to 25 megapixels so, eventually, you could wind up with even better vision. We would have to replace the photo sensor but that would be a relatively simple procedure. So, are you potentially interested?"

"Potentially interested? Potentially interested? Where do I sign?"

Dan broke in.

"Now, hold on just a second. You are talking about taking all kinds of things out of the eye and then putting all kinds of other things back in and then you are talking about all of that interfacing with the brain. I agree that, on the surface, this sounds fantastic but there are all kinds of things going on here. I'm especially concerned with this whole brain interface thing. What would be the potential risk to Jake?"

"I believe that the risk to Jake would be minimal. Of course, with any surgery, there is some risk of infection but that risk is low here. Regarding the brain interface, I suppose that, if some kind of power surge found its way to the brain, that could cause serious problems. However, I just don't see how that could happen. In fact, there is a current limiter, at the juncture between the interface circuitry and the optic nerve, which is designed to prevent such an occurrence."

"Does Vision Biotech manufacture the hardware that would be implanted?"

"No, we are developing the technology but we don't have the facilities to manufacture it. Building those facilities would cost more than what we have spent on developing the technology. We simply can't afford that at this stage. We are contracting out the manufacturing of the devices that will be implanted in the first procedure. If that procedure is successful, and we have every reason to believe that it will be, then we plan to take the company public. At that point, we will acquire our own manufacturing facilities. That is our hope anyway."

"I'm sure that, if the first procedure is successful, then you will have no problem raising capital in an initial public offering. I have been involved with the IPOs of a couple companies in the biotech field, which appeared to show less promise than your company does, and they had no problem attracting capital."

"You have been involved in biotech IPOs? If I may ask, what do you do?"

"I am a CPA. I use to own part of an accounting firm in Atlanta. I recently sold out and moved back to Jackson, which is where Jake and I are from."

"What are your plans now?"

Dan laughed.

"Well, I don't really know. I'm just sort of playing it by ear and seeing what comes along. I'm thinking of starting a consulting business but I'm not entirely sure."

Jake broke in.

"Hey guys, did you forget about me?"

Ben laughed.

"Oh no, Jake, I didn't forget about you. I'm glad to see that you are so interested in our technology. I would like to formally extend to you the offer for you to be the first recipient of this technology. Think about it. You don't have to make your decision today. In order to formally get things started, we would have to do an in depth eye exam and a neural exam. We have an ophthalmologist and neurologist on staff but neither of them is here today so the exams would have to wait anyway."

"OK, I'll think about it. I can already tell you what my answer will be but I'll think about it before I tell you yes."

"Excellent. Now, Dan, I'd like to talk to you about something."

Dan looked surprised.

"Me?"

"Yes. I think that there may be an opportunity here for you as well. Actually, it would be an opportunity for both of us. I told you that, pending the successful completion of the first implantation procedure, we intend to take the company public. If we are to do that, well before we actually get to the public offering, we are going to need a chief financial officer to make sure that everything is in order and to guide us through the process. You are a CPA, you have experience handling IPOs in the biomedical field, and, professionally, you are looking for something to do. From my side of the table, this potentially looks like a pretty good match. Is this something that you may be interested in?"

Dan sat there, deep in thought, for several minutes. Then, he spoke.

"Well, possibly. I have never been a CFO but I have performed a lot of CFO type work. In fact, providing CFO type services to small businesses is what I was thinking about doing with my consulting business, were I to start such a business. I had not considered trying to land a position as the CFO of a single company. However, I do have experience that is relevant to your situation. Also, helping to take a company public that is on the absolute leading edge of medicine sounds fun. I have been wanting to get away from all of the day to day drudgery and something like this might fill the bill."

"Excellent. So you may be interested then?"

"Yes, perhaps. Let me think about it."

"Oh yes, by all means. Both of you take your time and I hope to receive positive responses from both of you."

Ben saw them out. As they passed through the reception area, Christine was on the phone but she smiled at them as they passed and she waved at them as they got to the door. She was holding the phone in her right hand and she waved with her left hand. Dan noticed the lack of a wedding ring. He sure wished that he had gotten to talk to her more. There was just something about her. Oh well, it looked like both he and Jake might be spending more time around Vision Biotech so he might have plenty of opportunity to talk to her yet.

Chapter 13

As Dan and Jake left Vision Biotech, they were both in a very buoyant mood. As they walked through the parking lot, they were silent, each lost in his own thoughts. With Jake holding Dan's arm, they walked up to the passenger side of Dan's truck. Dan said "here you go". Jake let go of Dan's arm, extended his hand forward, and felt for the door handle. He opened the door, planted his foot on the running board, and, keeping his right hand on the door for balance, swung himself up into the leather seat. He felt for and put on his seat belt, while Dan went around to the driver's side.

As Dan pulled his door closed, they looked at each other and, simultaneously, said "can you believe that?" and then they both laughed at the fact that they had spoken simultaneously. By the time that Dan pulled out of the parking lot, they were deep in conversation.

"I never thought that there would be any chance of me being able to see anything again and especially not like this."

Shortly after Jake's premature birth, he had been screened for ROP, as was common for babies that had been born as prematurely as he had been. Through a detailed eye exam, performed by a retina specialist, it was discovered that he did have the beginning of the retinal scarring and other retinal damage that was diagnostic of ROP. The retinal deterioration continued until he was about three years old, at which time the ROP was said to have stabilized. At this point, he had ambulatory vision, or just enough vision to be able to get around without bumping into things, if he was familiar with the environment. He also could read print if it was magnified about 20 times by a computer or CCTV magnifier. He had kept this amount of vision until, at age 19, there was a string of complications, following cataract surgery, which took what little vision that he had.

"I would love to just get back what I lost following those cataract surgeries but I have always assumed that it would never be possible. Now, it looks like I might get back even more than that. Dan, I might be able to see close to the way that you see. I might even be able to drive. Can you imagine?"

In fact, Dan could not imagine. Only yesterday, hadn't he wished for this very thing? Not only yesterday, but countless times before, and yet, he had never thought that it would ever actually happen. It had seemed so far beyond current medical technology and even beyond the point where technology was likely to advance within their lifetime. And now, maybe, here it was. Dan couldn't imagine what Jake must be feeling.

"Jake, I am so happy for you. You know, you're right, if this whole thing is as good as they say that it is, one day, maybe, we will be making this same trip with you driving. Hey, in a few months, maybe we can go shopping for you a vehicle. What do you think about that?"

"That would be absolutely unbelievably awesome. For now though, how about we point this vehicle toward a place where we can get something to eat. I only had a bowl of cereal and a cup of coffee this morning and, with all of this excitement, I'm starving."

"Hey, sounds good to me. What do you have in mind? Fast food or something better?"

"Well, how about fast food. I am anxious to get back to Jackson. I want to tell Mom and Dad about this."

"Sounds good. McDonalds sound OK? There's one right up here."

"Sounds fine."

They pulled in and got their food. While they ate in the truck in the parking lot, they continued to talk. Between bites of his burger, Jake asked Dan what he thought of the possibility of becoming the CFO for Vision Biotech.

"I'm really not sure. On the one hand, I am qualified and it does sound exciting. On the other hand, I would probably need to move to Memphis and I'm really not sure that I would want to do that."

"Hey bro, that secretary, what was her name, she was very friendly and had a very pleasant sounding voice. She sounded pretty. If she isn't married, you moving to Memphis might not be that bad."

"OK, first of all, what do you mean she sounded pretty? How can someone sound like they look a particular way?"

"I can't explain it exactly but a person can sound like they look a certain way. Think about it. Doesn't Darth Vader sound ugly?"

Dan was taking a drink of his Coke and he laughed so hard that he spit half of it on the steering wheel and he aspirated the other half. When he finally managed to quit laughing and coughing, he said "oh man, this sure has turned out to be a great day".

"OK, I get your point. Well, just so you know, that secretary, her name is Christine by the way, she looks the way that she sounds. She is absolutely beautiful. It's a little hard to judge her height with her sitting down but I'd say that she's a little over five feet tall and weighs a little over a hundred pounds. She has long, straight, blond hair. She has very pretty blue eyes and a light complexion."

"Yes, she does sound pretty. And, on her left hand, was there a wedding ring?"

"Well, honestly, I didn't notice but no there wasn't."

"Oh, see, there you go. You need to find someone to replace Cathy. You have got to take that job as CFO. You can have a new career, new girl, new everything."

Dan was surprised by the fact that the mention of Cathy didn't bother him like it usually did. Especially, given that the mention of her name was in the context of replacing her with another love interest. After all, he had basically left Atlanta in an attempt to run from her memory. When he really thought about it, though, it wasn't really the memory of what they had had that troubled him, it was the thought of what they could have eventually had. But, really, could they have really had anything more? Things between them hadn't been good in a long time and she hadn't appeared to be interested in making them any better. Really, he supposed that he had lost her long ago. It was time to stop grieving that loss. It was time to start over, in every way.

"Well, bro, you know, I just might do that. Getting the girl may prove to be a little more difficult than getting the job but I might just try to get both."

They both were laughing as they pulled back onto the road and headed for Jackson.

"Seriously, Dan, it may be none of my business but that's never stopped me before so I'm going to say it anyway. I have always liked Cathy but, to me, she never really seemed all that in to you in the first place and the way that she just walked out on you, without any real reason or discussion, was pretty crappy. I think that you deserve someone better than her and I think that, one day, you will find them. Hopefully, it will be sooner rather than later. But, if it's going to happen at all, you are going to have to let go of Cathy and start looking for someone new, or, at least, be open to the possibility."

Dan was silent for a few minutes. It was Jake who broke the silence.

"Have I offended you? If so, I'm sorry, but that's how I feel."

"No no, you didn't offend me. I was just thinking how ironic your statement was because, back there, in the McDonalds parking lot, I was thinking pretty much the same thing. I need to start over, and not just where Cathy is concerned. I want something more exciting in my career too. I'm tired of the same old grind, day after day. Don't get me wrong, I have made very good money in accounting and I am thankful for that. I don't want to leave the accounting field entirely but I am ready for a change. I'm ready for something a little more challenging. Something where I feel like I'm making a difference."

"Well, sounds to me like taking that position as CFO of Vision Biotech is just the thing for you. And, if you really don't want to move to Memphis, it could probably be worked out so that you wouldn't have to. I mean, with a computer, a phone, and a fax machine, you could conduct business from Jackson just as easily as if you were in the office next door to Dr. Nelson. Come to think of it, that might actually work better because, unless he just didn't mention it, there wasn't an extra office in their facility that you could occupy anyway."

"Yeah, that's true. Hadn't thought of that. You're pretty smart, for a blind guy."

"Hey, you know, I'm blind, not stupid."

"Oh really? I thought you were both."

Jake punched Dan's arm and they laughed.

"You know what? To heck with it. I'm going to do it. Provided that I can set up my office in Jackson, I'm going to take the job as CFO for Vision Biotech. I'll call Dr. Nelson, when we get back to Jackson, and let him know."

"Great!"

"Now then, Jake, what about your decision?"

"What decision is that?"

"You know, the decision whether or not to take part in the clinical trial."

"Like I said, what decision? I told Dr. Nelson that I would think about it before I told him yes and that's exactly what I meant. Sure, I'm sure there are some risks. There always are. Sounds like they are minimal though. My eyes already don't work so what's the harm in letting them poke around in there? And there is so much to gain. I'd be crazy not to do it."

"Great! Sounds like we both have a call to make when we get back."

Chapter 14

James Swanson walked into his office at Biotronics, a small Memphis based manufacturer of biomedical electronics, where he was the head laboratory technician. He glanced around at the tiny, ten by ten office, which was crammed full of journals and equipment, which barely left room for his small desk and chair. He thought "at least I have an office, one of the few perks of this crummy head tech position". He flopped down in his chair and thought about the morning that he had had.

He had awakened, at 4:30am, to the cry of Jenna, his six month old baby girl, the youngest of his three children. He had testily said "what's wrong with her, she doesn't usually wake up this early". His wife, Beth, said "you know she hasn't been feeling good because she's cutting teeth". James sighed and said "oh yeah". Beth said "I'll get her", as she climbed out of bed.

As Beth trudged down the hall, James thought about his day ahead. He had to go into work early today, something that he did not look forward to. He did not like his job at Biotronics. He enjoyed the work but it didn't pay nearly enough, especially considering all of the administrative crap that he had to deal with. Six months previously, he had been promoted to head lab tech. That title came with a lot of administrative responsibility, a tiny office, and a one dollar per hour pay raise. He hated the administrative part of his job. He had to keep up with supply inventory and ordering, equipment maintenance, and scheduling, among other things. The tiny office and one extra dollar per hour didn't make up for all that crap. Besides, even with the extra dollar, he still only made $16 per hour, 33 thousand per year. That didn't go far when trying to support a family of five.

He thought "well crap, might as well get up". After all, he had to get an early start on the day anyway, although he hadn't planned on getting started this early.

He went into the bathroom and turned on the water in the shower. After a minute, he checked the water temperature. It was still ice cold. Crap! That darned water heater again. It intermittently quit working and the problem had gotten much worse lately. He was going to have to somehow find the money to get it fixed, along with about a dozen other things around here. That wasn't going to be easy, considering that he was barely managing to even make the house payment.

After taking a very quick, very cold shower, he got dressed and went into the kitchen, where he found Jenna in her high chair and Beth at the stove. Beth was trying to cook Jenna an egg.

"The front left eye isn't working again and the front right will only get up to about half temperature. To even get an egg cooked on this thing, I have to play musical eyes with the pan."

"I know, I know, I know! I'll add that to the list of all the other things that I have to get fixed around here when we win the lottery."

"We don't play the lottery."

"Well, maybe we had better start because I think that's the only way that we are going to get the money to do any of the things that we need to do around here."

"Maybe I should look for a job."

"Beth, we have been over and over this. Even if I wanted you to get a job, which I don't, it wouldn't make sense. We have three kids that we would have to put in daycare which would eat up everything that you would make. No, absolutely not."

"Well then, maybe you need to ask for a raise. They can't keep turning you down forever."

"Sure they can. Even if I were to quit, I wouldn't be that hard to replace and they know that. They keep telling me that they will give everyone a big raise, once the company really gets on its feet, but they have been saying that for three years, ever since the company started, and things really aren't looking much better than they were back then. I think that the only reason that they are able to make ends meet right now is this contract with Vision Biotech. We have worked with them on this technology that they are developing and we will manufacture the implants that will be used in the initial clinical trials but, after that, I think that they are going to take production in house. Who knows what will happen then. So, forget a raise. I'll be lucky to even still have a job in a year."

She came and kissed him.

"Well, if that happens, you will find something, maybe even something better."

She nibbled his ear.

He laughed and playfully pulled away.

"Stop that, we don't need a fourth child to have to take care of. By the way, I took a freezing shower this morning. Go ahead and call the plumber today. We have got to have hot water. Just put it on the credit card. Why not, we do that with practically everything else. I'll stop on the way to work and get a lottery ticket."

Now, as he sat at his desk and contemplated the morning, he was thinking about asking for a raise after all. Larry McDonald, the guy who owned Biotronics, was basically a good guy. Maybe if James explained the situation to him. His thoughts were interrupted by a knock on the door jam.

He looked up to see a man standing in the door way that he did not recognize. The man was perhaps six feet tall and weighed around 200 pounds. He had a full beard that was well groomed. He

119

was well dressed, wearing a white button down shirt and black slacks. He was also wearing sun glasses, despite the relatively low light in the office. For a moment, James tried to place him and could not, which was surprising. Not many people came into the facility other than employees and clients, both of which comprised a relatively small group of people, and almost all of which James knew.

James stood and extended his hand. The stranger reached out and shook.

"Hi, can I help you?"

"My name is Steve Levet. I am here to see James Swanson."

"I am James Swanson. Do you have an appointment? Please forgive me but I don't believe that I know you."

"No sir, I don't have an appointment and you don't know me. However, if I may, I would like to have a moment of your time."

"If you are a sales representative, I'm afraid that I don't really have time today. There is a project that we are falling behind on and I have come in early to work on it."

"Would that be the Vision Biotech project?"

James was a bit taken aback. The fact that Biotronics and Vision Biotech were working together wasn't exactly a secret but not many people knew about it. James spoke a bit tentatively.

"That is correct but how do you know about that?"

"Never mind that. I am not exactly a sales person but I think that I do have something that you will want. May we talk, in private?"

James hesitated.

"Well, yeah, sure."

James got up and moved a stack of journals so that he could close the door. There was no extra chair so Steve pulled up a sturdy looking equipment box and sat on it. James sat back down and looked across the desk at Steve.

"So, what's this about? You said that you are not a sales person but you have something that I will want. I am confused."

"Yes, I would imagine that you are. Let me explain. First of all, let me tell you what I have that you will want."

James was beginning to think that this guy was putting him on and, when he next spoke, his voice had a slightly amused tone.

"OK, what is it that you have that I will want?"

"I have 250 thousand dollars and, with your current financial condition, I am quite sure that you will want that."

Now, James was getting angry. How did this guy know anything about his finances? He didn't try to hide the anger in his voice when he spoke.

"Just how in the heck do you know what kind of financial trouble that I do or do not have?"

"Oh, I know a lot of things about you. I had to check up on you in order to make sure that you are suited for the job that I have in mind."

"Job, what job?"

"Hang on. I'll get to that in a second. Right now, just think about the payment for the job. Think about your house. That little dump that you bought for 100 grand back just before the real estate market tanked. Looks like you can't keep up with the repairs and you are having trouble making the house payment. Have you thought about selling? I'm sure that you have. The market is recovering but your house is still only worth, what, maybe 90 grand, at best. Less than that after you pay the real estate commission. And you owe what on it? About 95 grand? You couldn't get out of it even if you wanted to. But, after you do this little job for me, you could pay it off and fix it up real nice."

By now, James was livid. He stood, pointed at the door, and in a tight voice, said "get out".

Steve remained relaxed and totally calm.

"Now, just hold on, don't get upset. I'm just pointing out the advantages of what I am offering. Perhaps I did come on a bit strong there. I'm sorry about that. But, really, think about it. Think about what you could do with that money. You could pay off and fix up your house. Or, you could buy a new house. You could get Beth a new car to hall those little kids around in. A car that you wouldn't have to worry about breaking down all the time. You could stop hauling a set of jumper cables and a tool box in the trunk. Just think about it. Biotronics is never going to be your ticket to easy street. When the Vision Biotech contract is up, they may even go belly up. But, with this money, you wouldn't have to worry about that. You could take care of a lot of things and still have tens of thousands in the bank. For the first time, you would have some breathing room."

James had mostly calmed down. He had gotten past the shock of Steve's seemingly unlimited knowledge. He had started thinking about what Steve was saying and, no matter how he knew what he knew, he was right. James was drowning financially and Biotronics was not going to be the lifeline. Maybe he should listen to what this guy had to say.

"So, you are willing to pay me 250 thousand dollars to do what you call "a little job". Just what is this little job?"

"Not that much, considering what I would be paying you. My client has a vested interest in the failure of Vision Biotech. I want to sabotage the clinical trials and I want you to help me to do that."

James wasn't surprised. He knew that, for 250 thousand, it would be no small project. He hated to do that to Vision Biotech and Biotronics but Biotronics probably wasn't going to survive anyway. He had to start looking out for himself. He contemplated this for a moment before he spoke.

"Will anyone get hurt, other than financially I mean?"

"Oh no. I'm not in the business of hurting people. I only hurt companies, when they get in the way of my clients. We can work out the details later. For now, I just want to know if you are willing. In order to entice you, should you decide to accept this assignment, I have here a little something for you. Think of it as a signing bonus."

Steve produced a thick envelope and handed it over.

James opened it. It was full of cash.

Steve said "go ahead, count it".

James did. There was a thousand dollars, in twenties. He just sat for a moment, savoring the feel of it in his hands. Maybe they wouldn't have to put that water heater repair on the credit card after all. His lottery ticket was sitting right here across the desk from him.

Steve said "so, do we have a deal". James hesitated only slightly before he said "we have a deal", as he reached across the desk and shook Steve's hand.

Chapter 15

Christine pulled into the parking lot of Olive Garden and found a parking place. She switched off the ignition and as the relative silence washed over her, so did the fatigue. She had slept very poorly the previous night. She just couldn't get her mind to slow down after the incident with Roger. Right now, more than anything, she just wanted to take a nap.

Christine was here to meet Nancy Fletcher, the wife of John Fletcher, the man who had saved Christine from Roger. Nancy had called and invited Christine to lunch. On any other day, Christine would have looked forward to this lunch. She had lunch with Nancy about once a month and both women thoroughly enjoyed each other's company. Today, however, Christine was dog tired and she had a feeling that Nancy wanted to talk about the incident with Roger, which was something that she did not want to talk about.

Christine scanned the parking lot, looking for Nancy's car. About the time that she saw it, there was a knock on her window and she almost jumped out of her skin. It was Nancy. Christine opened her door.

"Crap! You scared me half to death."

Nancy hugged Christine.

"Oh, I'm sorry. I should have known that you would be jumpy, especially with that crap that Roger put you through last night."

"Oh, it's OK, really. Just give me a minute for my heart to slow down."

Nancy looked at Christine appraisingly and a look of concern came over her face.

"Christine, I mean this in the best possible way but, girl, you look like crap. You have dark circles under your eyes the size of the tires on your Explorer."

"I'm OK. Really I am."

"That's bullcrap and you know it but we'll talk about that later."

They went inside and waited for a table. They were right in the middle of the lunch rush so they had to wait for quite a while. While they waited, Christine talked about a couple of sewing projects that she was planning and Nancy talked about the latest antics of her and John's two kids. Finally, they were seated at a table.

While they waited to place their order, they continued their small talk. Nancy was talking about a promotion that John was hoping to get.

"I really hope that he gets it. It would mean a little more money and that would be nice, of course. It isn't just that though. He loves his job and he works so hard to provide for me and the kids. I think that this promotion would give him some renewed pride and sense of accomplishment. For a man like John, feeling that he is doing well at his job and providing well for his family is very important."

As Nancy spoke, the love that she felt for John shone brightly on her face. Christine felt a pang of regret that she didn't have someone in her life that she could feel that for.

Finally, the waiter came to take their order. They ate here frequently and so both of them already knew what they wanted. After they ordered, they got their salad and bread sticks and ate that while they waited for their entrees. For a few minutes, they ate in silence. After a while, Nancy spoke.

"John told me about what happened with Roger last night."

126

Christine thought "oh great, here we go".

"Yes, I assumed that he did."

"As I understand it, he didn't really hurt you. Is that right?"

"No, he didn't really hurt me. He just left a few bruises on my shoulder and scared the heck out of me."

"Yes, I'm sure that he did scare the heck out of you. John said that you were white as a ghost and shaking like a leaf. I think that I know the answer to this question just from looking at you but how did you sleep last night?"

"I didn't sleep well, maybe a couple hours. I probably wouldn't have slept at all if it weren't for the gun under my pillow."

"I'm glad that you have that gun. Are you going to start carrying it again?"

Christine patted her purse.

"I already am."

"Good. Very good. He has been calling more lately, hasn't he?"

"Yes, he has. I finally just stopped answering. I think that's what really set him off."

"His behavior is becoming ridiculous and obviously threatening. Are you going to try to get a restraining order? "

"No, I don't think so. I don't think that it would really do any good. I think it would just tick him off more."

"Yeah, as bad as I hate to say it, you're probably right. So, what now?"

"Well, I don't really know. I guess I just carry the gun, maybe get some pepper spray, and hope for the best. There's really nothing else that I can do."

"No, I guess not."

Their entrees arrived. The food was delicious and both women were hungry. They dug in and ate in silence for a few minutes. Then, Nancy spoke.

"I know that you don't really want to hear this but you really need to move on from Roger."

"I have moved on. I have no feelings for him at all anymore. Well, accept for negative ones. That was true even before I left him."

"Yes, I know that. That's not what I'm talking about. Because of the way that Roger treated you, you have trust issues with men, when it comes to romantic relationships. Now, I don't blame you for that. No one would. But, if you don't get past that, you will never be able to have someone special in your life. You are such a wonderful person and you have such a sweet spirit, even after what Roger did to you. I want you to have someone who you can love and who can love you back, someone who can make you as happy as John makes me. You deserve that."

Christine thought back to the pang of regret and sadness that she had felt earlier when Nancy had been talking about John. She had to admit that she wanted that. She wanted to have what Nancy and John had. She had to let go of what Roger had done to her. But how did she do that?

"Yes, Nancy, you're right. I haven't fully moved on. At least, I haven't moved on to someone else and, I have to admit that I do want that. How do I do that though? I can't just flip a switch and forget all of the things that Roger did to me and the way that he made me feel."

"You shouldn't forget the things that Roger did. Remembering those things will probably help you to make better choices next time and, when you do find the right man, you will appreciate him all the more. I don't know exactly how you do this. Think about it and pray about it. Are you still attending Faith Baptist Church?"

"Yes, I am. I don't make it to every service but I'm trying to do better about attending. I am a Christian but, in the past few years, I have drifted away from God, especially after the divorce. I'm trying to get back to him."

"Over the years, when I just don't know what to do, I have found that the best thing to do is to turn to God. Talk to your pastor. Maybe he can help you. He might be able to council you or refer you to a good Christian counselor. He can certainly pray for you."

"That's a good idea. I think that I will talk to him."

"Great. I'm glad that's settled. Now, finish your food. I think you've lost a little weight lately and no man likes for a woman to be too skinny."

They both laughed.

Christine had been sort of dreading this lunch but, now, she was glad that she had come.

Chapter 16

In the middle of the afternoon, Ben was working in his office, reviewing the latest reports concerning progress that was being made in the lab. The reports looked very good and he was very pleased. His thoughts were interrupted by Christine's voice coming from his phone.

"Dr. Nelson, Jake Richardson is on line one."

"Excellent. Thank you Christine."

He was in a buoyant mood as he picked up the phone.

"Hello, this is Dr. Nelson, how may I help you?"

"Dr. Nelson, this is Jake Richardson."

"Jake! Great to hear from you. And, I told you, call me Ben."

"OK, Ben. I'm calling about your offer for me to participate in the upcoming clinical trials."

"Good, I'm glad to see that you are thinking about it. Can I answer any questions for you?"

"No, I think I understand everything pretty well. I would like to accept your offer to participate."

"Excellent! Excellent! I'm so glad to hear it. Now then, we will need to make an appointment for you to come and get everything finalized. It will take a few hours. I will need to explain a few more things and you will need to get a detailed eye exam as well as a neurological exam. Then, of course, there's the paper work. I'll need a few days to get everything scheduled and set up. How does next Wednesday sound, at 9:00am? It will probably take most of the day."

"Next Wednesday? That sounds just fine. I'll have to talk to Dan, just to make sure, but I don't think that will be a problem."

"OK, great. After you talk to Dan, if that won't work, for whatever reason, just let me know and we will reschedule."

"Will do. See you next Wednesday."

"Yes, see you then."

After they hung up, Ben sat back and a feeling of contentment washed over him. The first part of the plan had just fallen into place. Now, if only the second piece would fall as well. As though his thoughts had prompted it, Christine's voice again came through the phone's speaker.

"Dr. Nelson, Dan Richardson is on line one."

"Excellent! Thanks."

"Hello, this is Dr. Nelson, how may I help you?"

"Dr. Nelson, this is Dan Richardson."

"Dan! Great to hear from you. And, as I just told your brother, call me Ben."

"OK, Ben. Yes, Jake was sitting right here when he called you."

"Ah yes, I am very excited about his decision to take part in our clinical trials. What can I do for you, Dan?"

"I want to talk to you about the possibility of my becoming your CFO."

"OK, Can I answer any questions for you?"

"Actually, yes. One concern that I have is that my family is in Jackson and I don't really want to move to Memphis. Would it be possible for me to serve as your CFO from Jackson? As Jake pointed out to me, in this age of information technology, I could do it from here almost as easily as I could do it from there."

Ben was very pleased at this. Though he hadn't previously thought of it, he had actually rather Dan do his work off premises. It would mean that there would be less chance of him stumbling across things that he did not need to see.

"Oh, yes, yes. I assure you that will not be any problem whatsoever."

"Great! In that case, I accept your offer. We can talk about compensation later. Although it's probably dumb of me to say this, honestly, the money isn't really all that important to me. I'm OK financially and I'm really looking for something exciting, challenging, and somewhere where I feel like I can make a difference. I think that this position will fulfill all of those requirements."

"That's absolutely fantastic. If you will be bringing Jake next Wednesday, we can just work out all of the details and finalize everything then. Sound OK?"

"I will be bringing him and that sounds great. I look forward to it."

"As do I."

After Ben hung up, he sat back and this time the feeling that washed over him was more than just contentment. It was pure elation. The second piece of the plan had just fallen into place. Now, there only remained the third part of the plan, which was to get Dan to invest in the company and he had no doubt that, with the first two parts of the plan firmly in place, this third part would work out as well.

133

He thought that, since everything was going so well, perhaps he should give Vinnie a call and let him know what was going on. It might take him down a notch or two on the ticked off meter. Perhaps not. Vinnie hadn't really encouraged much further communication the last time that they had talked and Ben didn't enjoy talking to him anyway. Still, it might be prudent. With some trepidation, Ben picked up the phone and dialed.

"This is Vinnie."

"Hey Vinnie, this is Ben Nelson."

"Ben! How are things in Memphis this afternoon?"

Ben felt a little better about the call. There was no trace of the anger that had characterized Vinnie's voice at the end of their last conversation.

"Oh, things are going just great in Memphis this afternoon. That's what I'm calling you about."

"Oh, really? Do tell."

"Well, do you recall me telling you that we had identified someone who would be perfect for the first clinical trial?"

"Yeah, sure I remember, the guy with the wealthy brother, right?"

"That's right. Both the guy and his wealthy brother came to see me and were very impressed with what we are doing. He has decided to take part in the clinical trial."

"Great. Does the wealthy brother seem to be supportive?"

"Oh yes, very much so. I have some good news regarding him as well."

"More good news? Well, aren't things just rosy for you? What is this good news?"

"Well, remember that we talked about taking the company public?"

"Of course."

"Well, in order to do that, we are going to need a chief financial officer (CFO) to get everything ready and to guide us through the process. The wealthy brother is an accountant who just sold out his part of a large Atlanta accounting firm and he's looking for something to do. I just hired him as our CFO."

Vinnie was silent for a few seconds.

"Ben, do you think that was wise?"

Ben was taken aback. He had not expected that response. When he spoke again, his voice was a bit more tentative.

"Well, yes, I do think it was wise. Why would it not be?"

"Think about it. You say that you need a CFO and I tend to agree with that. However, CFOs really dig into the financial records of a company. That's part of their job. In the case of a company like yours, with all that digging comes some risk, the risk that they will discover the relationship between our two organizations. A discovery like that is something that neither of us needs."

"Well, yes, that's true and I had already thought a little about that. However, as I have explained, in order to get through our, um, financial problems, we are going to have to take the company public relatively quickly. I just don't see any way that we can do that without the help of a good CFO."

"No no, you are missing my point. I just told you that I agree that you need a CFO. I don't really have a problem with that. It is your particular choice of CFO that I question."

"I'm sorry but I don't follow you. Do you know Dan?"

"Dan is it? No, I don't know him. The problem that I have is this. He isn't just some accountant that you found. He is the brother of the first patient in your clinical trial. Hopefully, you are about to bring sight to his blind brother. Also, hopefully, he is about to invest millions in your company. With all of that, he is going to take more than just a purely professional interest in your company so it is much more likely that he will stumble across something that we don't want him to stumble across."

Ben had worried a little about Dan but he hadn't thought about things in quite that way. Vinnie had a good point. Also, Vinnie knew that his point was good and he wasn't happy that Ben hadn't already thought of it. These things were beginning to make Ben nervous again. Crap! He knew that he shouldn't have called Vinnie.

"Well, perhaps Dan will be so wrapped up in what we are doing for his brother that he won't be paying as close attention as you may think."

"Yeah, maybe, but accountants tend to be logical people who don't get too terribly wrapped up in anything very easily. I guess we will see what happens but I sure hope that you know what you're doing Ben."

Vinnie said that last bit in a rather ominous tone. As at the end of their previous conversation, Ben's bowels again turned liquid. He just couldn't win with this guy.

Chapter 17

The next Wednesday morning, Dan and Jake arrived at Vision Biotech promptly at 9:00am. When they walked in, Dan immediately noticed that Christine looked much better than she had looked the last time that he had seen her. The dark circles under her eyes were gone and her smile seemed even more radiant. She said "good morning gentlemen".

Almost simultaneously, Dan and Jake said "I'm here to see Dr. Nelson".

Christine laughed.

"Oh yes, I know, everyone has been excited in anticipation of your arrival. This is so cool. Finally, we're getting into clinical trials. Not that I know that much about it. I'm just the receptionist but, still, it's very exciting."

She picked up her phone and announced them. No sooner had she hung up than Ben appeared in the doorway behind her. He rushed forward and vigorously pumped Jakes hand, then Dan's.

"Gentlemen, gentlemen, so good to see you!"

He led them down the hall, to the second door on the left, which was the break room.

"Sorry to have our initial meeting in the break room. There are five of us and none of the offices are very big and so I thought that it would be easier if we make initial introductions here. Grab you some coffee and a doughnut."

At the round table sat two people, a relatively short red headed woman and a medium to tall African American man, both roughly middle age and both wearing lab coats. Each of them was sipping coffee. They both stood upon the arrival of Dan and Jake.

Ben said "this is Mark Fleming, our ophthalmologist, and Rebecca Crowder, our neurologist.

Each of them shook Jake's and Dan's hands. Dr. Crowder said "pleased to meet you". To Jake, Dr. Fleming said "so, did you drive down here". Everyone laughed and Jake said "now I like that, someone who can joke about my blindness, you and I are going to get along just fine".

They all took a seat at the table and Ben spoke.

"OK, First, Dr. Fleming will perform a detailed eye exam. That will take quite a while, probably an hour or so, wouldn't you say, Mark?"

"Yes, I would say around an hour."

"Then, Dr. Crowder will perform a neurological exam. That won't take as long as the eye exam because it will mostly consist of taking a neurological history and just a very basic physical exam. How long would you say that will take, Rebecca?"

"I would say about 30 minutes."

"Yes, that's about what I thought. Then, I will explain a thing or two and we will do a mountain of paperwork. Sound OK, Jake?"

"Sounds fine to me."

"Great. Dan, while Jake is with Doctors Fleming and Crowder, you and I can finalize our business, if that's OK with you."

"Sounds good to me."

"Great. Let's get started then."

Dr. Fleming stood and allowed Jake to take his arm. Dr. Fleming said "let's go next door to the exam room" and they left.

Ben said "Dan, let's go to my office".

They sat down in Ben's office and, for a while, just made small talk, Ben talking about how momentous this step was, getting into clinical trials, Dan talking about how huge an opportunity that this was going to be for Jake. After about five minutes of that, there were several seconds of silence, after which Ben spoke.

"Well, let's get down to business, shall we?"

"Sounds great. I'm really excited about this."

"Excellent! You probably know much better than I what this job will entail so I won't try to really give you a big job description. You will oversee all financial record keeping, though Christine can do much of the clerical work for you. You will assist with all business planning. You will prepare the company to go public and you will guide us through the IPO. Of course, we will have a series of initial meetings in order to help to familiarize you with the company and, of course, all records will be open to you. Is what I have described about what you expected?"

"Yes, absolutely."

"Good. I just want to make sure that we are on the same page. I will leave the details to you as you are, after all, the expert. Now then, to the issue of compensation. We are on a relatively tight budget, as you will soon see for yourself. We would like to start you out at 75 thousand per year. I know that isn't much for this job but, once we go public, we can double or triple it. Do you think that you can tolerate such a low pay, just for a few months, until after the IPO?"

"Sure, that isn't a problem. As I told you on the phone last week, at this stage of my life, money just isn't that big a deal to me. I'm looking for other things."

"And I hope that you find what you are looking for working for us."

"As do I."

"I believe that we discussed that you would work from Jackson."

"Yes, that is what I would like to do, definitely."

"That works just fine for us."

"Good. How about this? Let's just do this on a contract basis, for 95 thousand per year, and I will take care of my own equipment, facilities, and such."

"Hey, even better. Makes the paperwork simpler too."

"It sure does. I'll draw up a letter of engagement and E-mail it to you for approval. Sound OK?"

"Sounds just great."

"OK, well I guess we're done here. That didn't hurt a bit."

"No, sure didn't."

The two men stood and Ben shook Dan's hand.

"Well, you basically work here now. No need for you to go back out to the reception area while you wait on your brother. If you like, go back into the break room and have some coffee. There are some newspapers and magazines in there."

"I think that I will. Thanks."

Dan went into the break room and got a cup of coffee. He sipped his coffee and flipped through a couple magazines. He wasn't particularly impressed with the available selection of reading material. He decided that he may as well do something productive. He went out to his truck and got his laptop computer. He brought it back into the break room and started to work on the letter of engagement, the document that would spell out the basic terms of service and compensation between himself and Vision Biotech. He became engrossed in his work and, before he knew it, almost two hours had passed and he had finished the document. He was very pleased that he had finished and he thought that he may as well go ahead and E-mail it to Dr. Nelson. In order to do that, he would need to log onto the company's Wi-Fi in order to establish an internet connection. When he tried to log on, he was prompted for a password which, of course, he did not know. He went looking for someone who could give it to him.

He went out to the reception area, which was empty accept for Christine. He said "can you give me the password for the Wi-Fi". She smiled but looked at him a bit uncertainly. He immediately understood the reason for her hesitation. He hit himself on the forehead and said "oh, of course, I guess you wouldn't know, I'm the new CFO for the company". Suddenly, Ben' voice came from the door behind him saying "indeed he is, give him anything that he needs Christine". Now she looked a bit sheepish. She said "yes sir" and gave Dan the password. She and Dan made small talk for a few minutes before Dan returned to the break room and finished his little project.

A short time later, Christine came in and took a small plastic container and a soft drink from the refrigerator. She sat down across from Dan and smiled warmly as she opened her drink and took out her sandwich.

"So, you're our new CFO?"

"Yep, sure am."

"Cool. I guess we will be working together then."

"Yes, Ben said that you would be helping me with some of the clerical work."

"Sure, I actually welcome a little extra work. I have a lot of down time and I often get bored anyway."

They sat in silence for several seconds before Christine spoke again.

"So, you are moving to Memphis then?"

"No, I will set up an office in Jackson and will work from there. My family is in Jackson and there is no extra office space here anyway."

"Oh yeah, I didn't think about the lack of office space. That's too bad."

Dan wondered what she meant by that.

"You said that your family is in Jackson. Do you have kids?"

"No, no kids. My parents and my brother live in Jackson. I am originally from Jackson but I have lived in Atlanta for the last 15 years. I recently went through a divorce and, after that, I decided that I needed to make a few changes. I just moved back to Jackson, just last week in fact. How about you? Do you have family?"

"No, I too am divorced, about three years ago. No kids, no boyfriend, not even a dog."

142

She laughed and Dan thought that the sound was one of the most wonderful things that he had ever heard. They continued to make small talk for several minutes. Then, Ben came in with Jake in tow. Dan had been enjoying talking to Christine and was sorry for the interruption in the conversation.

"Hey Dan, I got the letter of engagement that you E-mailed to me. That sure was fast. Now that's what I call initiative."

"I aim to please. Hey Jake, are you all done?"

"Yep, sure am. It went a little faster than I thought."

"So, are you ready to get on the road to Jackson? I might let you drive back."

Christine laughed and Dan was again enraptured by the sound, which made him not want to leave.

"Yes, I guess we may as well head back. We need to grab some lunch too. I'm starving. Are you done here Dan?"

"Sure am."

Jake took Dan's arm and they headed out the door, though Dan was certainly not ready. As they left, Christine smiled warmly at Dan and said "I'll see you around". Dan smiled back, just as warmly, and said "yes mam, you surely will".

Chapter 18

One week later.

Dan sat behind his new desk in his new office. He looked around at the sparse furnishings, which simply consisted of a large desk, the chair in which he sat, and two smaller chairs across the desk. He was eagerly awaiting the arrival of Christine, who was bringing him some material from Memphis. He was excited about the work that he was going to be doing for Vision Biotech and he was anxious to have the materials that he would need to get started. However, that wasn't the only reason that he was looking forward to Christine's arrival. He also just wanted to see her again. He had found himself thinking about her a lot in the last week since he had last been in Memphis.

The day after he and Jake had gone to Memphis, Dan had gone in search of suitable office space and had found this place. It was a little more space than he really needed. There was a small reception area, which he wasn't using, two offices, a kitchen, and a bathroom. He didn't need the reception area or the second office but the rent was relatively cheap and, he thought, who knows, he might set up a work space in the other office for Christine. If she was going to be helping him with clerical work, it could come in handy to have her here for some projects. And besides, it might be pleasant just to have her around some. He couldn't believe that he was thinking about wanting to have her around just for the heck of it but he supposed that that was a good sign for him.

His thoughts were interrupted by a knock at the front door of the building. He got up and walked out of his office, through the deserted and unfurnished reception area, and opened the door. There stood Christine, looking as radiant as ever in a t-shirt that said "Go Vols" and blue jeans. Her hair was in a ponytail. She said "excuse my casual appearance but I thought that you could use some help with getting everything set up and so I thought this would be better".

145

He said "oh, yeah, sure, no problem, I'm sure that you would look beautiful in anything". He was immediately embarrassed that he had said it, especially when he saw her blush. He said "I'm sorry, it's just that, well, you are quite beautiful and, well, I think I'll shut up now before I make a bigger fool out of myself". She laughed in her musical way, smiled warmly, and said "no problem, you don't make a fool of yourself just by complimenting a woman".

She followed him into his office and they both sat down. She took a USB flash drive out of her purse and laid it on the desk.

"Most of the material that you will need is on that."

He picked it up.

He said "all digital records, you could have just E-mailed this". He then quickly added "not that I would have wanted you to".

"No, E-mail wouldn't work. There's 23.8 gigabytes of data on that."

Dan laughed.

"Oh, OK, I guess E-mail wouldn't work too well for a set of files that large."

"No, it sure wouldn't. Also, there are several boxes of files out in my Explorer."

"OK, I'll help you get them."

They brought in the file boxes and stacked them along one wall of the unused office. As Dan was getting the last box out of Christine's Explorer, he saw a large three ring binder lying beside the box.

"Is this binder for me too?"

"I assume that it is. Dr. Nelson helped me to load the boxes.
They were in his office. That binder was lying on top of one of the
boxes, the last box that I picked up. I just assumed that it was for you
and that I should bring it."

Dan thumbed through the binder.

"Yeah, it probably is for me, there are some financial records
in here."

Dan laid the binder on top of the box and took it into the office
where all of the other records were. Slightly out of breath, he spoke.

"Man, I'm glad that was the last one. Those things were
getting heavy. We're getting quite a collection in here. I might want
to scan and digitize all of this. It sounds like most of the records are
digital anyway and it would make everything much easier to deal
with if everything is digital."

"Yes, it sure would make it easier. Scanning all of this would
be quite a job. I can come back and help you with that, if Dr. Nelson
says it's OK."

"He better say it's OK or I'll quit."

They both laughed.

"So, is that it?"

"Yep, that's it. Do you need anything else?"

"No, I don't think so. I would like to get all of this scanned
but I don't have a scanner that is suitable for this much volume. I'll
get some more equipment and talk to Ben about you coming back for
a day or two. Is that OK with you?"

"Yeah, sure, sounds great."

Her face lit up with another one of those radiant smiles.

Dan looked at his iPhone and checked the time. It was 11:45.

"Hey, would you like some lunch before you head back?"

"No, I had better not. I would like to but I got the impression that Dr. Nelson wanted me back pretty quick. I'll just get something and eat on the way back."

"OK, well, we can do lunch when you come back to help me scan all these records."

"Sounds great."

Dan saw her to the door and, as soon as she left, he called Ben and arranged for her to come back the next day to help him to scan the records. As he hung up, he thought "I'm going to like this job even better than I thought".

Chapter 19

Jake sat in his study, in front of his computer. He had just finished a long stretch of writing. He had very recently started writing the novel that he had been planning. He was finding writing very difficult today. He had been writing all day and he had only produced about 500 words. He was so preoccupied with the situation with Vision Biotech that he was finding concentrating almost impossible. He thought "Jake, old boy, you are going to have to do better than this".

He decided that he may as well take a little break from writing and see if that would improve his concentration. He wanted some coffee and he went into the kitchen and started the coffee brewing. While he was waiting, he decided to check his E-mail. He had only one new E-mail, which was from Dan.

In the E-mail, Dan explained that Christine had just brought the records from Vision Biotech and that, because there was so much material, he might need some help in reviewing everything and getting up to speed. Dan said that most of the records were already digital but that there were several boxes of files that were not. He said that Christine was coming tomorrow (Thursday) to help him to scan those records so, by Friday, everything should be digital. Dan asked if Jake would mind spending a day or two with him at the office, helping him to go over the records. Dan said that he felt that Jake would be very good at this, given his own CFO experience, and offered to pay him $25 per hour. Jake replied that of course he would be glad to help out and that he was looking forward to it.

Jake got his coffee and sat down in his study, sipping the coffee and thinking about Dan. He was very pleased about what he thought might be a budding relationship between Dan and Christine. From what little he had been around them and from what Dan had said about her, it was obvious to Jake that Dan and Christine were somewhat taken with each other. He hoped that a romantic relationship would develop there. Christine seemed like a very nice person and he thought that Dan deserved some happiness.

After a few minutes, his thoughts turned to helping Dan to review the records. Dan had said that most of the records were digital but he hadn't said exactly what form they were in. If they were standard document formats, such as Microsoft Word, Microsoft Excel, PDF, and such, Jake could just review them on his laptop. However, if some sort of accounting or management information system was needed to access the records, Jake might have to use one of Dan's computers because he would not have the necessary software on his laptop. He decided that he may as well make a copy of JAWS, his speech software, in case he ended up needing to install it on one of Dan's machines. He reached into one of his desk drawers and took out a blank USB flash drive. He plugged it into his laptop and copied the necessary files. He then used his Braille label maker to make a label with a J, for JAWS, and he stuck that label on the flash drive. He then put the flash drive in his computer bag.

With that task done, he went and got another cup of coffee and he settled in in front of his computer for another attempt at writing.

Chapter 20

When Dan awoke on Thursday morning, for the second day in a row, he sprang out of bed, ready to start the day. He dashed for the bathroom, brushed his teeth, and jumped in the shower. As he showered, he thought about the day ahead.

He would be spending the day scanning boxes and boxes of records. This would be a very tedious task and one that he would normally be dreading. However, Christine would be coming from Memphis to spend the day helping him. He thought that this should turn the day from a mind numbingly boring experience into a very enjoyable one. He was actually looking forward to the day and he couldn't wait to get started.

He jumped out of the shower, dressed quickly, and dashed downstairs. He didn't even take the time for a cup of coffee. He said a quick good morning to his parents as he dashed out the door.

Dan arrived at his office at 7:00. He went to get things ready in the room in which they would be scanning the records. The previous afternoon, he had purchased two high volume document scanners with high speed document feeders as well as two new laptops with very fast processors. He had also purchased some very powerful document scanning software which was designed to scan a large amount of documents, perform optical character recognition (OCR), and create standard document files, such as Word or Excel files. He had spent much of the previous evening getting everything setup and tested. All of the equipment was sitting on a long folding table, which he had also purchased the previous day. The scanners were at each end of the table with the laptops in the middle. The file boxes were stacked, on the floor, to either side of the table. He turned on the equipment and went through a quick check to make sure that everything was in order.

He then sat down at his desk to wait for Christine. She was supposed to be there at 8:00. He had tried to tell her that it wasn't necessary to arrive so early, especially since she had to drive from Memphis. She had said that they had a lot of work ahead of them and that they may as well get an early start. At 7:30, Dan heard a knock at the front door of the office. He wondered who it could be as Christine wasn't supposed to be there for another 30 minutes.

When he answered the door, he found Christine standing there with a big smile on her face and a big McDonald's bag along with two steaming cups of coffee in her hands.

"Hey, you're early."

"Are you complaining?"

"No no no no no. Actually, I'm glad. Hey, that smells delicious."

"I haven't eaten yet and, while I was getting my breakfast, I thought that I might as well get you something too. Have you eaten?"

"No, actually, I haven't. Thank you. That was very thoughtful. What are we having?"

"I didn't know what you would like so I got two sausage biscuits and two bacon biscuits."

"I like both so take your pick and I'll take whatever is left."

"That's sweet. Let's each have one of each."

"Sounds perfect."

They laid the food out on Dan's desk and sat down and began to eat.

"This sure hits the spot. The coffee is great too. I have a coffee pot here but I haven't taken it out of the box yet. Thanks again."

"No problem. Glad to do it. Did you get us some scanning equipment?"

"I sure did. It's in the other room with the files. We each have a work station set up for scanning. I got everything set up last night. I scanned the contents of that three ring binder to test everything. It works great."

"Oh, that reminds me. Dr. Nelson wants me to bring that binder back today. That wasn't actually for you."

Dan shrugged.

"It looked like it was for me. I didn't look closely but there were definitely financial documents in the binder. No big deal though."

While they finished eating, and for a while afterword, they made small talk, talking a little about their families and their past. At about 8:00, Christine said "well, I guess we had better get started". Dan agreed and they went into the other office.

"Hey, I am impressed. When you said that you had us some scanning equipment, you weren't kidding. These scanners look like they could do the job without any help from us. These laptops look top of the line too."

Dan laughed and said "well, may as well do it right, no need in messing around".

Christine placed a finger on the touch pad of one of the laptops to clear the screen saver, revealing the scanning software.

"Wow! I've used this software, at my previous job. This stuff can do absolutely anything, as far as document scanning is concerned. We are set!"

Dan laughed again.

"Well, I'm glad that you are familiar with it. That should make things go much faster."

They set to work and quickly settled into a routine. The automatic document feeders could take 500 pages at a time. These were very fast scanners but, still, it took several minutes to scan a stack of pages that size. This gave Dan and Christine a lot of idle time, just sitting there, looking at the computer screens. As the scanners worked, Dan and Christine talked.

Christine had never talked much about the situation with Roger, especially not to a man. However, for some reason, she felt very comfortable with Dan. She found herself opening up to him about a lot of things, including Roger. She told him about the courtship, the marriage that quickly went wrong, and about her eventually leaving him. She even told him about her problems trusting men enough to date again and about her recent determination to overcome that hurtle.

Similarly, Dan had never talked much about his situation with Cathy but he too found himself opening up. He told Christine about desperately wanting a child that was never to come and about the heartbreaking slow loss of Cathy's affection. He told her that he had basically come back to Jackson in an attempt to get away from the memories in Atlanta. He told her that he too was recently determined to move on and find someone.

Dan had a problem with the scanning software on his computer. After a couple minutes of trying to fix the problem, frustrated, he said "what's wrong with this darned thing". Christine said "here, let me". As she leaned over his shoulder to get at the touch pad, he could feel the heat radiating from her skin and he could smell her perfume. He found himself feeling desires that he hadn't felt in a long time.

At around noon, they appeared to be about half finished. Feeling that they were making good progress, they decided to break for lunch. Though they were making relatively good progress, they knew that they didn't have time for a sit down lunch. They decided on McDonalds again. Dan said that it would be his treat this time and they went in his truck to pick up the food. They brought it back to the office and again ate at his desk.

They made a little small talk, as they ate, but Dan was oddly quiet. He wasn't eating all that much either. He looked a little uncomfortable and, eventually, Christine asked him if he was OK. He said that he was. After a couple more minutes of relative silence, he put down his burger and spoke.

"Christine, the reason that I am so quiet is that I want to say something and I can't figure out how best to say it. So, I may as well just come on out with it. Ever since the first day that I saw you, a couple weeks ago at Vision Biotech, I have been taken with that radiant smile and musical laugh of yours. Over the last couple days, as I have gotten to know you a little, I have found that you are just about the nicest, warmest person that I have encountered in quite a while. I find myself thinking about you all of the time. I think that I sense a little attraction from you too, at least I hope so. We have both been talking about moving on. Well, let's try moving on together. Christine, would you go out with me?"

Now, Christine put down her burger as well. She looked a bit stunned. Dan worried that he had screwed things up. He knew that he had said too much, more than he had intended. Still, he didn't think that he had expressed himself that badly. Perhaps she just wasn't interested. Perhaps he had offended her, though he didn't

155

think that she was the type to become offended by someone asking her out, even if she wasn't interested. After what seemed like an eternity of silence, Dan spoke again.

"OK, now it's my turn to ask if you are OK. Have I offended you?"

"No, you haven't offended me at all. It's just that no one has asked me out in so long. Not since my college days. Roger and I got married right after college and then, after we divorced, I wasn't interested in dating, as I've told you, and I guess that guys could sense that. Actually, Dan, I'm flattered. I am attracted to you too. Honestly, I had hoped that something might eventually develop between us. I hadn't thought about anything happening this soon but, what the heck, yes, I would love to go out with you."

She treated him to yet another radiant smile and musical laugh. Actually, this laugh was more of a giggle, which was even more musical to Dan's ears. He was so excited, more excited than he could remember being. He thought "now, how am I going to get any work done this afternoon" but work they did, even more efficiently than they had in the morning. At first, Christine was rather quiet and Dan feared that he had screwed up after all but, by midafternoon, Christine was seemingly bubbling over with excitement and, seeing this, so was Dan.

"Hey Dan, where should we go, and when?"

"Well, let's figure out when first. How about Saturday night?"

"Sounds great."

"OK, that was easy."

They both laughed.

"You have driven to Jackson twice in two days. On Saturday, how about I come to Memphis?"

"I won't argue with that."

"OK, great. Now, let's see, what to do. Memphis has so many things. You live there, you suggest something."

"Well, I have wanted to eat at the Rendezvous for a long time. I have lived in Memphis for all these years and have never eaten there. How about that?"

"Sounds great. I've never eaten there either. Pick you up at 5:00?"

"Sure. Looking forward to it."

"Me too!"

She gave him directions to her apartment. They were finished with scanning the documents at about 4:30. He picked up the binder and said "don't forget this". She took it and thanked him. He walked her to the door and, just as she was about to leave, She stood on her tiptoes and kissed him lightly on the cheek. With yet another radiant smile (she seemed to have an endless supply) she said "I'll see you Saturday night".

Chapter 21

The sound of a bell tower filled James Swanson's bedroom. He reached over to his iPhone and silenced the alarm. The sound had not awakened Beth, who lay sleeping beside him. He felt good. Baby Jenna had slept through the night and they had gotten the first really good night's sleep in a long time. He lay there and pondered the last two weeks as well as the day ahead.

It had been two weeks ago that he had met Steve Levet. In the time since then, he had tried to comprehend exactly what he had gotten himself into. James had always considered himself to be a relatively moral person. He had never cheated on Beth. He did his part to help her to raise the kids. He paid his taxes. He occasionally went to Church. He was no boy scout but, all in all, he thought that he was an OK guy. But now, it felt a bit like he had sold his soul to the devil. Larry, the owner of Biotronics, was basically a good guy. James didn't think that Larry paid him enough but that was hardly a crime and sabotaging the Vision Biotech project was almost certainly going to put Biotronics out of business. The company employed 12 people, all of which would lose their jobs. He couldn't help but feel a little guilty about that.

On the other hand, he thought about the money. He thought about it a lot. In the past two weeks, he had gotten the water heater and the stove fixed. He had made the mortgage payment, which was almost a month late. And he still had $100 tucked away in his wallet, just in case something else came up. Beth would certainly not have understood if she had known where the money had come from. He had told her that Larry was finely beginning to recognize that he was overworked and underpaid and he had given him a bonus. He felt a little guilty about that too but what was he supposed to do? He couldn't tell her the truth. He had no idea how he was going to explain the 250 thousand that was coming but he would figure it out.

Yesterday, he had received a text from Steve saying that he wanted to meet with James today to "discuss the project". James assumed that, today, he would find out more about exactly what this "project" would involve. He figured, whatever it would involve, it would be worth it. Steve was to be at Biotronics at 8:00. James looked at his phone. It was 6:15. He decided that he may as well go ahead and get the day started. He smiled as he thought about a shower with plenty of hot water.

He sat down at his desk at 7:45. Unable to concentrate, he pushed some papers around his desk, while he waited for Steve. Promptly at 8:00, Steve walked in and closed the door. It annoyed James slightly that Steve had such a presumptive attitude but he said nothing. Steve extended his hand.

"So, James, how have you been the last couple weeks?"

"Just fine."

"I trust that you have put that signing bonus to good use?"

"Oh yes, I surely have."

"Good, good. Today, I would like to get more into the details of our little project."

"I assumed as much. What exactly do you have in mind?"

"Well, I will leave the exact details to you. Let me tell you specifically what I want to accomplish."

"OK, I'm listening."

"As I told you previously, my client has a vested interest in the failure of Vision Biotech. I want to sabotage the clinical trials. I want to create in incident related to the implant that will reflect very badly on Vision Biotech. I want to be absolutely clear about this. I don't want this to be just a little bump in the road for them. I want potential patients and investors to be scared to even come near them. So, basically, I want a catastrophic outcome."

James stammered a bit.

"But, you said that no one would get hurt, other than financially."

"Did I say that? Perhaps you misunderstood me."

"No, I don't think so."

"Well, it isn't that big a deal. I mean, the patient doesn't have to die. They do at least need to suffer though. Like I said, I want some very bad press here."

James had turned pale and was completely silent. He hadn't expected anyone to get hurt, at least not badly. Seeing his trepidation, Steve offered a bit more enticement.

"OK, I can see that you are very uncomfortable with this. I am willing to try to help you out here. Perhaps I was a bit unclear in our initial meeting. Would another hundred thousand increase your comfort level? And remember, the patient doesn't have to die. There don't even have to be any long term effects. I just want potential patients and investors to stay away long enough for the company to dry up and blow away, which shouldn't take very long, given their precarious financial condition. Come on, what do you say?"

Some color returned to James' face and he appeared to relax a little.

"OK, as long as the patient doesn't die and isn't permanently harmed."

"Excellent. Now then, how do you propose to accomplish what I want?"

James was deep in thought for several minutes. Then, on his computer, he pulled up several design schematics and studied them intently. After a while, he spoke, a bit tentatively.

"I could modify the brain interface device. If a power surge found its way from that device to the brain, that could cause serious problems, probably a seizure. There is a current limiter, at the juncture between the interface circuitry and the optic nerve, which is designed to prevent such an occurrence. I could disable this current limiter and then modify other circuitry to cause a power surge."

"You believe that this is a realistically viable option?"

After studying the information on his computer screen a bit more, James said, with more confidence, "yes, I am quite sure that this is doable".

"Excellent, excellent. And have I sufficiently calmed your fears concerning this?"

James thought for a moment.

"I am going to be honest. I am not nearly as comfortable with this as I was 30 minutes ago but I will do it."

"Good."

As he had done at the end of their previous meeting, Steve produced a thick envelope and wordlessly handed it over. This time, James knew what would be inside and he was correct. Another thousand in cash. The feel of it in his hands calmed him a bit more.

Steve stood to go.

"I want you to make plans to get this done. When next we meet, I want for you to be able to tell me for certain that this is doable and exactly how you plan to do it. I think that they are close to clinical trials so we will probably need to move on this soon."

James nodded. Steve shook his hand and left.

Chapter 22

Friday morning, Jake sat in a rocking chair on his front porch with his computer bag in his lap. He was waiting for Dan to pick him up. Today, he was going to help Dan to go over the records of Vision Biotech. He was very excited about this. Not only would he be able to earn a little extra money but he very much enjoyed this type of work, though he hadn't done much of it since his days as the CFO of Discount Furniture. He wished that he could get another job like that but people were not anxious to give a blind man a job doing work of that sort because they didn't understand how he would be able to do it. Perhaps, if the implant procedure that was to be done by Vision Biotech were to be a success, he would be able to get another job as a CFO.

Soon he heard the clatter of Dan's diesel engine as he came down the street and pulled into the driveway. Before Dan had a chance to get out, Jake bounded down the steps, went down the walkway to the driveway, and hurried around the truck, lightly trailing his right hand along the body of the truck for guidance. He quickly felt for and found the door handle, opened the door, and hopped up into the seat. Dan said "I know that you get tired of hearing this but it always amazes me how you do things like that". Jake said "why, don't you know how to get in a truck too". They both laughed.

When they arrived at Dan's office, Jake told Dan that he had brought everything that he might need, including a copy of JAWS to install on one of Dan's computers, if needed. Dan explained that all of the records that he had in mind for Jake to look at were in the form of Excel and Word files so Jake should be able to just use his laptop. Dan said "why don't you go explore a little bit and get familiar with the place and then you can get set up in the other office". Jake spent a few minutes walking around the building, trailing his hands along walls, stopping to feel of furniture and other objects, making a map of the place in his mind. After a while, Jake called to Dan.

165

"Hey, what's with these two cool laptops and these two huge scanners?"

"Oh, those. I bought that stuff for Christine and me to use to scan some documents from Vision Biotech."

Dan summarized the specs for the computers and scanners. Jake was impressed.

"Boy, I'd like to have one of these things."

"Well, you know, now that I think about it, I don't really need them, at least not both of them. It was just a one day scanning project, which was finished yesterday."

"You bought this stuff for a one day scanning project? Were you trying to impress Christine or something?"

"Hey, knock it off. I doubt that Christine is all that impressed with fancy computers. Everyone isn't a nerd like you. By the way, Christine and I are going out tomorrow night."

"Hey, cool! Way to go! I'm excited for you. So excited that I will forgive you for calling me a nerd."

"Well, you are a nerd. Hey, would you like to have one of those computers? They are probably better than the laptop that you have. You can have one of the scanners too. I know that you scan a lot of documents and books, so that you can read them, and I bet you could make good use of nice scanners like these."

"Could I ever make use of them! Thanks. Give me a few minutes to get JAWS installed on one of these and I'll get started."

"OK, no problem, I'll be in my office. Just let me know when you're ready."

Jake sat down at the table, in front of one of the computers. He found the power button easily enough. He turned it on and, when he heard the Windows start-up sound, he used the key combination that would run the simple Windows built in screen reader, called Narrator. Once Narrator was running, he put in his USB flash drive and used Narrator to locate the JAWS installation program. Once he had the JAWS installer running, he closed Narrator. In just a few minutes, he had JAWS installed. He removed the flash drive and laid it aside.

He called to Dan and told him that he was ready to get started. Dan brought him the flash drive that Christine had brought from Memphis and he explained about its contents.

"This flash drive has a ton of data on it. I mean a ton, about 25 gigabytes. There's the stuff that was already in digital form, which was most of it, and it also has the stuff that Christine and I scanned yesterday. There is no way that you have time to look at all of it and you don't need to. For now, just look at the financial statements and see if they look to you like they accurately represent financial performance. If something doesn't look right, look at the general ledger to see if you can figure out what's going on. I doubt that you will need them but the subsidiary ledgers are on there too, along with the various registers. All of the things that you will be looking at are in Excel so you shouldn't have any problems with accessibility."

"OK, sounds good. I'll let you know what I find out."

Jake put in the flash drive and copied the entire contents to a directory on the hard drive, so that he wouldn't have to always keep up with the flash drive. He then browsed through the files. Dan wasn't kidding, there was a ton of data. There were financial statements, ledgers, registers, copies of every financial document, including invoices, checks, contracts, absolutely everything. He was impressed at how comprehensive the data was. He thought "well, I'll certainly have access to everything that I need, and then some".

He began by going over the statements of income for the past five years, all the way back to the company's inception. Dan wanted him to decide whether the statements accurately represented the company's financial performance and condition. After spending an hour or so with the documents, Jake sincerely hoped not. The financial picture that the statements painted was not pretty. Jake then spent a couple hours going over some other documentation, trying to decide whether the company's financial condition really was that bad or whether the company was reporting inaccurate operating results because of faulty accounting procedures. To his dismay, he concluded that the statements were accurate and that the company's financial condition really was that bad.

After reaching this conclusion, he went back to the statements themselves, trying to get a feel for the overall situation. The company had an alarming cash burn rate. In the first three years, they had gone through three million dollars, a million dollars per year. Then, the burn rate had doubled, increasing to four million dollars in two years, two million dollars per year. It looked like the burn rate was still increasing. In the past two months, the company had gone through about half a million dollars, which would equal an annual burn rate of three million dollars.

The most troubling part was not the cash burn rate but rather the funding, or lack of funding, that supported it. For the first three years, the company's capital needs had been funded by grants. Then, after the company almost went broke, an investor or lender, Jake couldn't really tell which, saved the company with two capital infusions, totaling four million dollars over a period of two years. The name of this investor or lender appeared to be HRC. Jake had never heard of them. Perhaps Dan had. In any case, it appeared that HRC was no longer willing or able to provide funding for Vision Biotech. The last infusion of capital had been 15 months ago. Three months ago, the company had begun to drown in red ink. Currently, they owed about 50 thousand dollars to various suppliers of lab equipment, 100 thousand dollars to Biotronics, and their primary checking account was overdrawn by about 16 thousand dollars.

He was beginning to get a sinking feeling in his gut as he pondered what the financial records were showing him. Dan stuck his head in and asked if Jake wanted to go get some lunch. Jake had lost his appetite and he said that he would rather keep working on this. Dan said "suit yourself, I am going to get something, I'll be back shortly".

Jake sat back and pondered the situation. From what he had seen in the financial records, it appeared that Vision Biotech was in trouble. From what he had been told, the implantation procedure wouldn't take place for at least a couple months. Given what he had found, how was the company going to even survive that long?

When Dan got back, Jake said that he needed to talk to him. They sat down at Dan's desk and, while Dan ate, Jake told him what he had found. Dan thought for several minutes before speaking.

"You are certain that the financial statements are accurate?"

"Well, I'm as certain as I can be, given that I have only had a few hours with them. I have looked at the statements themselves and a lot of the supporting documentation. Everything appears to be in order. Of course, you would be the better judge. I am not a CPA. However, I can say that, if there are any big problems with their accounting procedures, they are not obvious. I think that the financial statements that you gave me do paint a relatively accurate picture of the situation, albeit not a pretty picture."

"OK, thanks. I'll take a more in depth look but I'm sure that you are right. After all, you are pretty good at this stuff."

For a few minutes, both men were lost in thought. Then, Dan spoke.

"If you are right, then the question is, what do we do about it?"

"What do you mean, what do we do about it? What can we do about it?"

"I'm not sure. Let me take a look at the situation and think about it. Do you want me to take you home? You can work on your book and get your new laptop all set up the way that you like it."

"Yeah, sure. I will enjoy playing around with my new laptop and scanner. I need something to cheer me up."

"Oh, don't worry about it. Everything will be fine."

Chapter 23

At 4:00 on Saturday afternoon, Dan was in his truck, on I-40, headed to Memphis. He was full of conflicting emotions. He was overjoyed at the prospect of seeing Christine but he was also distressed over the things that he had learned about Vision Biotech. As he drove, he pondered the situation.

He had spent the previous afternoon and evening, as well as much of the day today, going over the financial records of Vision biotech. He had confirmed Jake's impressions. The company was, indeed, in trouble. He thought it strange that the financial condition of the company had not been pointed out to him when he had become CFO. Of course, it was possible that Ben did not really know the financial condition of the company. Dan had seen many cases in which owners or management of companies, of all sizes, really did not have any idea how the company was doing, financially. He had also seen many cases where the owners and management knew exactly what was going on and they just chose to ignore it, assuming that everything would work out, somehow. He supposed that this could be the case here. Whatever the case, as he had told Jake, the question now was what to do about it.

Obviously, the company needed a source of funding. As he understood it, Jake's implantation procedure would be done in about five or six months. The company was currently going through cash at the rate of about 250 thousand dollars per month. At that rate, they were going to need about 1.5 million, just to make it until the procedure, and that was if the cash burn rate didn't increase. Then, of course, there was whatever cost would be associated with the procedure itself. Dan figured that, in total, Vision Biotech was going to have to quickly come up with at least two million dollars in order to survive long enough to get into clinical trials. They might need as much as three million. It appeared as though their most recent source of funding was no longer willing or able to participate. Dan assumed that, if another source were available, the company would have already availed themselves of it. Of course, he would have to confirm all of this with Ben but, based on what he knew so far, it was a pretty safe bet. So, where was the money going to come from?

He could think of only one solution. He would have to invest or loan them the money. He wasn't entirely sure how he felt about that. On the one hand, he wasn't sure that he wanted to sink so much of his fortune into a venture that was already on shaky financial ground and whose technology was, as yet, unproven. On the other hand, if the procedure on Jake were to be successful, proving the technology, then the potential returns would be almost limitless. Then, there was Jake. Vision Biotech was offering Jake probably the only chance that he would ever have for close to normal eyesight. If Dan chose not to help the company, then Jake's procedure would most likely never happen. Regardless of the personal financial ramifications, Dan just didn't know if he could do that to Jake.

Dan was still tormented by these conflicting thoughts as he approached Exit 25. As he pulled onto the exit ramp, his thoughts focused on Christine and his spirits lifted. He had already put her address into the navigation app on his iPhone and he followed the directions that it provided. As he made his way to her apartment, he grew more and more excited at the prospect of seeing her again and getting to spend time with her outside of a work setting. Slowly, the thoughts of the problems surrounding the situation with Vision Biotech faded to the back of his mind.

He had no trouble finding her apartment. She met him at the door wearing jeans and a white blouse, with her hair in soft curls, cascading over her shoulders. Her look was very simple but nice. He couldn't get over how beautiful she looked, no matter how dressed up or dressed down she was. They stood there and made a little small talk, after which Dan motioned to his truck and said "your chariot awaits". She giggled, said "why thank you sir", and got in. When he started it and she heard the clatter of the diesel engine, she laughed and said "this is the loudest chariot I ever heard, but I like it".

When they arrived at the Rendezvous, it was already crowded and they had to wait for a table. While they waited, they talked. She asked how Dan liked living in Jackson, after so many years in Atlanta.

"Well, it has taken a little getting used to. Although I grew up in Jackson, I had become accustom to life in a much bigger city. You know, it's amazing how things change. When I was younger, I thought that I just had to get out of Jackson. I had big plans and I thought that Jackson was too small for those plans. I went off to Atlanta, married someone who I thought was a wonderful woman, and started a business that was successful beyond anything that I had ever envisioned. Then, I lost the wife, sold the business, and here I am back where I started, geographically at least. I like Jackson. Probably should have never left. After all those years in Atlanta, running R and R, a smaller town and a slower life appeals to me."

"I know what you mean. I'm from Huntingdon, which is much smaller than Jackson. I married Roger right out of college and we moved to Memphis because that's where his Dad's construction company was. After everything with Roger fell apart, I thought about moving back to Huntingdon. I like Memphis fine but I too would prefer a smaller, quieter town. Also, I'm pretty close to my parents and Huntingdon is where they still live."

"So, why didn't you? Move back I mean."

Christine sighed heavily.

"Well, I have a business degree, from UTM. I would like to eventually do something with it, not sure what though. Perhaps business planning consulting. I actually like working at Vision Biotech but I don't want to be a receptionist for the rest of my life.

You know? I thought that there would be a lot more opportunity for me in a city like Memphis than in a town of four thousand."

"Yes, that's true. Maybe you would like Jackson. It's much smaller than Memphis but much bigger than Huntingdon. It would be quieter but would still offer you plenty of opportunity."

Christine smiled. She had never really thought about Jackson.

"Hmmm. I hadn't thought about that. I would be closer to my parents too."

Dan smiled too.

"Well, you see, there you go. If you ever do decide to get into consulting, I would be happy to help you out. I have business contacts all over the south that could probably help you and I'd be happy to put you in touch with them."

Christine laughed.

"Oh, that's just a dream. I might do it one day but probably no time soon."

They continued to talk. Dan was enjoying himself immensely but the talk about professional matters had pushed his thoughts back toward the situation with Vision Biotech. They got a table and, after they had ordered and were waiting for their food, Christine noticed that he seemed somewhat preoccupied. She asked if everything was OK.

"Sure, everything is fine. Why?"

You suddenly seem a little distant. Are you having a good time?

"Oh yes, I'm having the best time that I have had in ages. I love being here with you. I just have something on my mind that is bothering me."

"Do you want to talk about it?"

"No. Well, maybe. OK, yes."

She laughed.

Dan thought for a few seconds about what he wanted to say.

"How much do you know about Vision Biotech?"

At first, she spoke a bit slowly and tentatively, as though she hadn't expected this to be the subject of Dan's concerns.

"Well, actually, I probably know less about them than you do. I have only worked there for about a year. I greet people, answer the phone, and do basic clerical work. Nothing that would give me any inside information. As the new CFO, I'm sure that you know much more than I do."

"I am just getting started in my role as CFO. As you know, I just got the company's financial records a few days ago. I have started going over those records and I don't like what I'm finding."

Christine looked surprised.

"What are you finding?"

"OK, first of all, this has to remain just between you and me. It isn't even ethical for me to be discussing it with you, given that you are not an owner or management and there is no reason for you to know this information. Actually, I can't believe that I'm talking to you about it but there is something here that is really bothering me and I need to talk to someone. I haven't known you for very long but

I feel like I can talk to you. You seem to be a woman of high morals and well thought out opinions. I would like to hear your thoughts concerning this."

"I'm flattered that you value my opinion and I assure you that whatever you tell me will remain in the strictest confidence."

"OK, great."

Their food arrived.

As they ate, Dan told her of his concerns. He told her about the financial condition of the company and the fact that, in order to survive, they would need capital that they apparently did not have access to. He told her about his thoughts concerning he, himself, providing the money that they would need. He told her that, in the end, he wasn't really sure that he had any choice, given that this was probably Jake's one and only shot at having eyesight. After he told her everything, she sat, deep in thought, for several minutes.

"So, how much money are we talking about here?"

"Without more information than I currently have, it's hard to say for sure. Probably somewhere between two and three million."

When she next spoke, she did so very slowly and tentatively.

"So, you have three million dollars?"

"Yes, I don't talk about that sort of thing much but I actually have much more than that."

She looked a bit stunned.

"Listen, Christine, the reason that I haven't told you about my money is that I didn't want it to influence your opinion of me, one way or the other. When people know that you have money, they sometimes see you differently. I wanted you to get to know the real me. Can you understand that?"

She thought for a minute.

"Yes, I understand it. Actually, I like it that you didn't tell me. For our first date, you came to pick me up wearing blue jeans and driving a truck that sounds like a meat grinder. You took me to eat barbequed ribs. You have millions, yet you didn't try to dazzle me with all of the things that you could afford. You seem to be just a regular guy who, it just so happens, has money. I like that. In fact, I like that a lot."

Dan laughed.

"Now look, leave my meat grinder truck out of this. I must be the only person in the world who actually likes the way that a diesel engine sounds. As far as my being just a regular guy with money, I'm not sure what regular means but I can tell you that money doesn't mean that much to me. It has never meant as much to me as it did to my former business partner and, as the years go by, money means less and less, although I accumulate more and more. Kind of ironic, I guess."

"Back to the topic at hand, have you discussed this with Jake?"

"No, it was Jake who initially discovered the financial condition of the company so he knows about that but I have not discussed with him the possibility of my providing the needed capital."

"Why not?"

"For one thing, he is hardly in a position to be objective. For another thing, if I do provide the capital, I don't want him to feel guilty that I would largely be doing it because of him."

"Yes, I see your point."

"So, what do you think?"

She thought for a long time.

"Well, it's easy for me to give advice concerning this because it isn't my two or three million and it isn't my brother. Having said that, this is what I think. Although I don't understand all that much about the science behind what Vision Biotech is doing, I think that there is a good chance that they will be successful, based on the sheer brilliance and dogged determination that I have seen in those who are working on the science. That isn't based on objective facts but that's my opinion. If the technology is successful then, from a financial prospective, it would be probably the best investment that you could make. Given Jake's involvement, from a personal prospective, I don't know that you could live with yourself if you don't step in. To me, your choice seems clear."

Dan pondered for a few minutes.

"Yes, you're right. It is clear. I guess I just needed someone else to tell me that. Thanks."

"No problem. You knew what you had to do. I just made sure that you listened to yourself. Now then. That was absolutely delicious and I'm tired of talking about Vision Biotech. Want to take a stroll down Beale Street, maybe listen to some Memphis blues?"

"Sure, sounds great. Let's go."

Chapter 24

On Monday morning, Ben sat behind his desk, smiling at his good fortune. He had just hung up the phone with Dan. He had been expecting the call from Dan ever since last Wednesday, when Dan had received the records. Finally, this morning, Dan had called. At first, Dan had simply said that he had a matter of great importance that he wanted to discuss and he wanted to schedule a time to discuss it face to face. After a little prodding by Ben, Dan had gone ahead and said what he wanted to say over the phone. He had told Ben of his concerns and his proposed solution. Ben had, of course, readily agreed. Ben had apologized profusely that he had not made Dan aware of the situation sooner, making the excuse that, this close to clinical trials, he had gotten so caught up in the research and testing that he just wasn't paying that much attention to financial matters these days. Dan had appeared to accept the explanation easily enough. As far as Ben could tell, there should be clear sailing from here on.

Ben decided that he should probably tell Vinnie, much as he hated to. He also decided that he would not tell Vinnie about the notebook that had gone missing for a couple of days. That notebook contained some information that Dan did not need. Ben had carelessly left it on top of a file box. As a result, Christine had loaded it, along with the other records. However, at his prompting, she had brought it back the next day. Dan had said nothing about it and so Ben assumed that he had not looked at it. So, no harm done and there was no need for Vinnie to know about it, just so that he could overreact and ruin this great day. Ben lifted the receiver and slowly dialed. The phone rang only once before Vinnie picked up.

"Hello."

"Vinnie, this is Ben Nelson."

"Ben, how are things in the fine city of Memphis this morning?"

"Things are great here and I have good news."

"Oh? Do tell."

"I just talked to Dan Richardson, our new CFO and the brother of the first clinical trial patient. He has seen for himself the financial condition of the company and, without prompting, he has decided to provide the needed capital."

Vinnie said nothing so Ben pressed on.

"He is about to send a cashier's check for 2.5 million, in exchange for which he will receive a 10% share of the company. In addition, we will have the option of a 500 thousand dollar loan, should it become necessary. He is about to draw up the agreements and E-mail them to me for my review."

"So, it will not be just a loan? He will have a stake in the company?"

"Yes. More potential return that way. I felt that was the best way to make sure that he stays onboard with the idea long enough to get the deal executed."

"That may be but it will also give him a greater personal interest in the company. As I said before, Ben, I sure hope that you know what you're doing."

"I am quite certain that I do."

"OK, well, as long as you get the desired result and I get my money, I don't care how you handle it. Thanks for the update."

"You're welcome."

"Good bye, Ben."

"Good bye, Vinnie."

As Ben replaced the receiver, he smiled. That had gone better than he had expected. He supposed that he was getting more used to dealing with Vinnie. This time, when Vinnie had ominously said "I sure hope that you know what you are doing", Ben had kept his composure and had not gotten sudden onset diarrhea. Today, nothing was going to ruin his day. Not even Vinnie. Ben whistled as he opened his E-mail program to see if he had received the documents from Dan.

Chapter 25

Vinnie sat in his office and pondered the situation. He had just spoken with Ben and he had mixed feelings about what he had learned. He was glad that Vision Biotech was going to get the money that it would need in order to survive. After all, he had 15 million riding on the future of the company. Much as Vinnie disliked Ben, he didn't really want to have him killed. He just wanted his money. The money was why Vinnie was here. Although this could, at times, be a violent business, Vinnie didn't particularly enjoy the violence. However, just because he didn't enjoy violence, that did not mean that he hesitated to employ it, when needed.

Unfortunately, he thought that it might end up being needed, in this case. He was very troubled by the fact that Vision Biotech's new investor was also the CFO and this same man was also the brother of the first clinical trial patient. As he had tried to tell Ben, Vinnie thought that this made for a very bad, and potentially dangerous, combination. He decided that it was time to start putting in place a little insurance policy against the trouble that might eventually arise.

He picked up the phone and called Barry Orsini. Barry answered after several rings, just before it went to voice mail. As always, his voice was very gruff.

"Hello."

"Why did it take you so long to answer?"

"I was target practicing and had my hearing protection on. It took me a second to hear the phone ringing and another little bit to put down the gun and answer. Don't bust my chops. What's up?"

"When you get a chance, come see me. No rush, just sometime today. I have a possible future project that I want to discuss."

Barry sounded a little annoyed.

"Be there in 30 minutes."

Barry abruptly hung up. Vinnie shook his head as he replaced the receiver. Generally, he did not tolerate such disrespect. However, to a limited degree, he tolerated it from Barry because he was good at what he did, which was to convince people to do what Vinnie wanted and, if convincing didn't work, eliminating them.

About 45 minutes later, Barry strolled into Vinnie's office and settled his large, 6 foot 4 inch and 300 pound frame into the chair across the desk from Vinnie.

"Took you long enough."

"I told you, don't bust my chops. What's up?"

"What does your schedule look like for the next month or so? What do the other guys have you doing?"

"Not that much on my schedule these days. I have a couple payments that I have to go collect every week. Not much fun. They never resist. Why? You got something better?"

"Yeah, maybe, not sure. I may need you to go to West Tennessee and rough up an accountant."

"An accountant? Is he involved in some of our money laundering?"

"Not directly."

"Does he owe us money?"

"No."

"Then why do you want him roughed up? Not that I really care."

"Let's just say that he works for a guy who does owe me a lot of money and I am afraid that he is going to stick his nose where it doesn't belong."

"You want me to remove his nose so he can't do that?"

"No, I don't want you to do anything right now but I do want you to keep your schedule flexible, your bag packed, and your cell phone on. This guy hasn't actually done anything yet but I have a feeling that he will and, if he does, I want you to be able to go do something about it quickly."

As Barry got up, he exhaled loudly.

"Yeah, sure. Sounds like fun."

After Barry left, Vinnie chuckled to himself. He was glad to have that taken care of.

Chapter 26

Three months later.

Dan sat behind his desk and stared at his computer screen. He leaned back and rubbed his eyes. It had been a long day. He was tired and was getting a headache. He decided to take a break and make some coffee. As he got up and went into the kitchen, his thoughts drifted back over the events of the previous three months.

Personally, the last month had been absolutely wonderful. The romance between him and Christine had quickly blossomed. They had gone out every weekend and, recently, they had begun to talk on the phone every night. She had also come to Jackson a couple of times to help him out with some clerical work and getting to see her a little extra had been really nice. They were getting pretty serious pretty quickly. His parents had not met her yet and his mother had begun talking about inviting her to dinner. This was fine with Dan but it had made him start thinking more seriously about finding another place to live. If he and Christine were going to be seeing each other long term, which appeared very likely, he was going to want more privacy.

Professionally, the last three months had been grueling. After Dan had gotten the money to Vision Biotech, he had set about getting the company's books in order. Actually, their records and financial statements were in surprisingly good shape, considering that, until now, they did not have anyone routinely monitoring their accounting procedures. However, there were faulty procedures and sloppy methods being used in some areas. Dan had set about finding and correcting these things, as well as correcting the resulting errors in the records and statements. It was very tedious work. He had been working 12 hour days, five days a week. On Saturdays, he only worked for eight hours, so that he would have time to get to Memphis and pick up Christine for what had become their weekly date. He was finally almost done with this phase of his work and he was ready to move on to something less monotonous. He was really looking forward to getting things ready for the IPO, which, hopefully, would occur right after Jake's procedure.

He had only one chore left to perform with regard to getting the past financial statements in order and he sighed heavily as he sat back down at his desk and contemplated it. In the past two and a half years, the company had two very large cash injections which were not properly accounted for in the records. In addition, the expense related to the facilities that the company now occupied was not accounted for at all. Dan had asked Ben about both of these things. Regarding the cash influx, Ben had said that these were loans but he was unable to tell Dan the terms of the loans nor was he able to provide Dan with the documentation regarding them. Regarding the facilities, Ben had said that the building was leased for ten thousand dollars per month but he was not able to produce the documentation regarding the lease and Dan could find no record of the lease payments having been made. Given that the company's books had been in relatively good shape upon Dan's arrival, he was very surprised and frustrated at these large errors or oversights or whatever they were.

He sighed again as he began to scroll through the documents that he had at his disposal that might help him to figure this mess out. He had already looked in all of the normal places, to no avail. He was stumped but he had to figure it out somehow. He had all of the company's financial documents on his computer, including the documents from the flash drive that Christine had brought him and all of the documents that they had scanned.

As he scrolled, a file caught his attention. It was labeled "Red Binder". For a moment, he was puzzled as to what the contents of the file would be. Then he remembered the red three ring binder that Christine had brought, along with the other files. He had scanned the contents of the binder as a test of the scanning equipment. He didn't know what the binder had contained so he didn't know whether or not the answer that he was seeking might be in this file. He hesitated before clicking on it, remembering that Ben had asked Christine to bring the binder back to Memphis, saying that it wasn't for Dan. Then Dan thought "what the heck". After all, he was the CFO and he was now also a part owner, having invested 2.5 million dollars in the company. He certainly had a right to see whatever the file might contain. He clicked on the file to open it and browsed through its contents. As he scrolled and read, under his breath, he slowly said "what the heck".

Chapter 27

Saturday evening, Christine sat in her apartment, excitedly awaiting Dan's arrival. While she waited, she thought about the last month and how her life had changed in that period of time. Looking back, it now seemed that her life, before meeting Dan, had been woefully incomplete. Previously, she had enjoyed her job and she had a few friends, like Nancy, that she occasionally enjoyed spending time with. However, she had never looked forward to seeing or talking to someone so much. She had never had someone who made her feel giddy, just thinking about them. She had never had someone with whom she felt comfortable talking about absolutely anything. It had never even been that way with Roger, even before things went so wrong. She felt like a better person, just having Dan in her life. She had never felt this way and she loved it.

Her thoughts were interrupted by a knock at the door. Her heart leapt. When she answered the door, her sudden giddiness was replaced by a slight sense of unease. Dan had a concerned look on his face. She was at once a bit apprehensive. Had she done something to displease him? She couldn't think of what it could be. Tentatively, she spoke.

"Hey stranger. You look, I don't know, concerned. Did I do something wrong?"

"Do something wrong? Oh, no no no. I just have something that is weighing very heavily on my mind. You are the best thing in my life right now. The best thing that has happened to me in a very long time. If not for you, I would feel much worse than I do right now."

Christine chastised herself for worrying so easily. She supposed that this automatic reaction would be with her for a while yet. It was a wound that Roger had left that would just take time to heal. Her pastor had said that it would take a lot of time and prayer to work through this. Apparently, he was right. She breathed a sigh of relief but then was immediately apprehensive about what had Dan so concerned. She kissed him and asked if he wanted to talk about what was bothering him.

"Yes. Can we sit down?"

"Sure."

She sat on the sofa and he sat beside her.

"I'm afraid that I have another concern about Vision Biotech."

"Oh no. If you want to talk about Vision Biotech then it must be serious. With all of the hours that you have been putting in, working on the books, you haven't even wanted to mention the name Vision Biotech when we have been together, not that I blame you."

"Yes, it is serious. Have you ever heard of the Petrillo Crime Family?"

"No."

"I'm not surprised. I guess, in the world of organized crime, they are pretty small. Anyway, I think that Vision Biotech has gotten mixed up with them."

Christine was flabbergasted.

"Vision Biotech? Associated with organized crime? How? Are you sure? How?"

"I am not entirely sure but I am about 90% sure. I had better start at the beginning."

"Yes, I think that you had better."

"Do you remember me recently telling you that I basically had just one big chore left to perform in getting the books all straightened out?"

"Yes."

"OK, well, that remaining chore was sorting out some problems related to the accounting for a couple of large loans and some lease transactions. I started looking for the documentation that I needed in order to correct the problems. I found the documentation. I wish that I hadn't."

"You said that you had to go looking for the documentation. Was it not included in the stuff that I brought to you?"

"It was included in something that you weren't supposed to bring to me. That red three ring binder."

"The red binder? But, I took that back the next day."

"Yes, you did but, remember, I had already scanned it as a test of the new equipment. So, I have it but Ben doesn't know that I have it, which is probably a good thing."

"Well, what is 'it'!"

"It is a set of documents that sheds light on the loan and lease transactions."

"Oh, OK, that clears it right up."

"Let me explain."

"Please do."

"Vision Biotech has received loans, totaling four million dollars, from a company that the regular financial records refer to as HRC. I saw that when you first brought me the records and I didn't

193

think anything of it. However, one thing that I found out by looking at the contents of the binder is that HRC was just an abbreviation for High Risk Capital. High Risk Capital is a front for another company that is a front for another company that is a front for the Petrillo Crime Family."

"How in the world did you come to know that?"

"When I was getting my certification in forensic accounting, I had to study all about different ways that fraud can be committed and has been committed, including money laundering and loan sharking by the major and minor crime organizations. The Petrillo Crime Family is one of the very minor crime organizations. I'm surprised that I remembered any details about them, especially such a small detail as the name of one of their fronts."

"Why would Dr. Nelson get the company involved with such an organization?"

"At the time of the first loan, Vision Biotech was very strapped for cash. Their third grant had run out. They apparently couldn't find any more grants or investors. It can be very hard to find someone who will take a chance on a startup company like this. The potential returns are quite high but so are the risks. Apparently, somehow, an opportunity came by that Ben couldn't pass up. Apparently, the Petrillos had some money that they were looking to launder and Ben's situation with Vision Biotech gave them the perfect opportunity to do that and earn some huge returns as well."

"You said that you are 90% sure about this. Why not 100%?"

"Because the information about the Patrillo Organization that I am basing this on is pretty old. I got my forensic accounting certification over five years ago. These crime organizations change things around all of the time, in an effort to keep law enforcement guessing. So, the company called High Risk Capital that was associated with the Petrillo Crime Family may be long gone and this one may be a totally different company. I doubt it though. The repayment terms are ridiculous. I don't think that any legitimate company would ever set up something like this."

"So, how do we find out for sure?"

"I don't know. There isn't a "Front for Crime Families" directory. I only know what I do about it because, when I was studying forensic accounting, one of my professors was a former FBI agent who had worked to catch money launderers and loan sharks. He had access to information that wasn't exactly classified but certainly wasn't generally available. I can try to find my notes from that class to see what else I can learn."

"If this can be confirmed, what are you going to do?"

"I don't know. I can't let an IPO go forward when I know that the company is using dirty money and I certainly can't take part in such an IPO. If I interfere, a few things will happen. Without taking the company public, in order to get additional capital, the company will not survive. The Petrillos will be very unhappy because they will lose their money. As a result, me, you, and my family will be exposed to great danger. Also, Jake's procedure will not happen and he will lose what will probably be his only shot at normal vision. I suppose that I, myself, will lose a couple million but that's the least of my concerns."

"Well, as far as Jake is concerned, if you do find out that your suspicions are justified, you can just wait to do whatever you are going to do after the procedure is done. You said that the company wouldn't go public until after that anyway."

"Yes, I guess that's true."

"Besides, there's no point in getting too worked up about this until we find out for sure that what you suspect is true."

"How are we going to prove it? I don't have the documentation that I would need. I'm sure that it's locked up tight at the Vision Biotech facility and, because I don't work at the facility, I won't have an opportunity to try to get it."

"That's true but are you forgetting that I do work at the facility?"

"No way! I am not going to ask you to do that."

"Then I am volunteering."

"No! Absolutely not! You do understand that I am talking about organized crime here? You know, like as in the Mob. These people are dangerous, very dangerous. They have a great investment and money laundering scheme going here. They put in some dirty money and get lots of clean money out. They will go to great lengths to protect their interest."

"Look. This situation does scare me. It scares me a heck of a lot. But I have also come to care for you a heck of a lot and you are knee deep in it. If you're in it, then I'm in it too. I'm not arguing about it and I won't take no for an answer."

As she spoke, there was a fire in her eyes that Dan had not seen before and there was a look of determination on her face that left no room for doubt or argument.

Chapter 28

James sat and stared at the device that sat on his desk. Its appearance was deceptively simple, a little half inch square which was about an eighth of an inch thick. The front of the device was black and contained a small rectangular socket into which a plug could be inserted in order to connect the camera. The back appeared to be solid gold but, in reality, contained over a thousand microscopic gold connectors which would connect to nerves in the optic nerve bundle. Despite the simple appearance of the device, it contained some of the most advanced micro circuitry in the world. It was the Vision Biotech neural interface device, one of only two in existence. Its designation was VBTI1L, the interface device designed for the left eye. Its sister device, VBTI1R, for the right eye, was still locked in the vault in the lab, from which this device had been taken about 15 minutes previous. James hoped to have this device back there soon. Having it out made him very nervous.

He had been putting this off for a while, both because of some misgivings concerning what he was doing and fear of being caught. Now, he could put it off no longer. Work on the interface devices was finished. They were scheduled to be delivered to Vision Biotech, within the next day or so, so that they could work on finalizing their work related to the implantation procedure. Actually, he supposed that it was a good thing that he had waited this long to sabotage the device. If he had done it any earlier, there was a chance that one of the other techs would have discovered the changes. There was very little chance of that now that the device would be delivered within a matter of hours and especially given that he was only sabotaging one of the devices, the implant for the left eye. This knowledge helped to ease his anxiety somewhat.

He had arrived at Biotronics at 6:00am. He wanted to have this little chore completed long before anyone else arrived. Theoretically, sabotaging the device should not be all that difficult. He would not have to actually make any physical alterations. He would simply have to make a couple of adjustments. This would not be complicated, thanks to the advanced design of the device. Uploading new software as well as changing settings was accomplished through a standard wireless Bluetooth connection. Anyone with the necessary software on their computer could manipulate the device. As the head lab tech, he did have access to the software, although manipulating the device's settings was not within his normal area of responsibility.

On his computer screen, he clicked on "VBT Interface" and waited for the program to load. He was then presented with several options. He clicked on "establish interface". He was then asked which device that he wanted to connect to. The software could manage the implant cameras as well. He clicked on "left neural interface (VBTI1R)" and waited for the connection to be made.

He was then presented with a vast array of options and parameters that could be configured. First, he unchecked the box for the current limiter. He was presented with a box, asking if he was sure that he wanted to do this. He answered "yes". He then went into the signal parameter options. He changed the signal strength from 30 micro volts to 800 micro volts. He was warned that this value was outside of the safety parameters and was asked if he was sure. He answered "yes". He then saved the settings and closed the connection.

With this chore done, he was in a hurry to get the device back into the vault, before anyone noticed that it was gone. Nevertheless, he again sat and stared at the device for a moment. It was amazing that such a small and simple looking device held so much potential and, at the same time, could do so much harm. He couldn't help feeling bad about what he was doing. After all, he didn't know for sure what would happen when the device delivered its much too strong signal to the brain. Hopefully, the patient would just have a seizure but worse could happen. Thinking about this, he almost undid what he had just done. Then, he again thought about the money. He had a family to support. He had to do what he had to do and he would just have to put thoughts of the patient out of his mind. Before he could think any more about the situation, he quickly grabbed the device, placed it into its protective container, and returned it to the vault.

Chapter 29

Christine sat at her desk and tried to calm herself. She had a very nervous feeling in the pit of her stomach. Actually, she felt like she was about to throw up. She had to get herself under control.

She and Dan had put together a little plan for her to obtain the documents that Dan would need in order to confirm his suspicions about Vision Biotech and the Petrillo crime family. It wasn't really detailed or specific enough to be called a plan. She was basically just supposed to go into Dr. Nelson's office and snoop around. Although Dan did have some idea as to what documents that he was looking for, there was no way to know where they would be kept or how they would be stored. They might be in another red binder on his desk, in a filing cabinet, or on a flash drive in a drawer. She thought "this is hopeless", as she tried to get herself under control. Although she had no idea how she was going to find what she was looking for, she felt that she had to try.

Today, Dr. Nelson had gone out for lunch, which was something that he rarely did. He was going to meet his fiancé for lunch so Christine assumed that he would be gone for at least an hour. There wasn't going to be a better time for her to snoop. She had spent the last 15 minutes just sitting there, trying to get up her nerve. She chastised herself, telling herself that, if she was going to do this, she had to get started, before she ran out of time.

She grabbed her purse and slung it over her shoulder. Reluctantly, she pushed herself up from her chair. There was no one in the waiting room and no one was expected. Doctors Fleming and Crowder were in today but both were working in the lab, preparing for Jake's upcoming implantation procedure. Christine went through the door behind her desk which led into the hallway where the offices were located. She didn't see anyone. She quickly turned to the right, went into Dr. Nelson's office, and shut the door.

She stood for a moment and let her heart slow and let her eyes adjust to the darkness. She didn't want to turn on the light. In case Dr. Crowder or Dr. Fleming came down the hall, she didn't want them to see a light under the door and come in, thinking that Dr. Nelson was in. After her eyes adjusted, she could see well enough with just the light coming under the door from the hall.

She sat down at the desk. There were several papers strewn across its surface. She couldn't easily read them in the dim light. She got a little pen light from her purse and used it to quickly examine the papers. They all looked like documents related to ordinary daily operations, such as research findings and procurement of lab supplies. She tried to leave all of the papers in the same position that she found them in. She looked through all of the drawers. She found only the usual mish mash of pencils, pens, and miscellaneous office supplies.

Just as she turned to examine the credenza, she heard footsteps coming down the hall and her heart leapt into her throat. Then, she heard the bathroom door open, across the hall, and her heart slowed, a little, and she silently prayed "Lord, please don't let me get caught in here".

She looked through the drawers in the credenza, again finding nothing of consequence. Her attention was then drawn to the laptop computer that was sitting on top of the credenza. The screen was dark. She placed a finger on the touch pad, to bring the machine out of standby mode. She fully expected to be presented with a request for a password. To her surprise, the desktop appeared on the screen. She couldn't believe her good fortune. She began to browse through the various available directories, having no real idea what she was looking for. Dan had told her to look for anything having to do with "High Risk Capital" or "HRC". After several minutes of searching, she was ready to give up and go back to her desk, before she was caught. She didn't know how much time that she had but she had been in the office for about 30 minutes and she figured that she was starting to push her luck.

Suddenly, there it was, a directory called "HRC". She clicked on it and a list of about 40 files appeared. Now what? She hadn't thought to bring a flash drive. She had no idea which of these files Dan might need. She did the only thing that she could think of to do. She created a Zip file, containing all of these files, and E-mailed it to herself. Then, she went into the "sent items" folder and deleted the sent E-mail. She then deleted it from the "trash" folder.

Just as she was closing the E-mail program, she heard someone walking up to the office door. Reflexively, she slid out of the chair, onto the floor, pushed the chair to one side, and slid backward, ending up about half way in the knee space of the desk. No sooner had she come to rest in this position than she heard the door open and someone walked up to the desk. Her heart almost stopped and she prayed "Lord, please protect me". Was it Dr. Nelson? She heard someone place a stack of papers onto the desk and she was somewhat relieved. Dr. Nelson probably wouldn't come back from lunch with a stack of papers. It must be Dr. Fleming or Dr. Crowder, leaving something for Dr. Nelson. She was still worried though. What if they came around the desk? There was no way that they could miss seeing her there. And what if they had noticed the computer screen with the HRC information still on it? It probably wouldn't mean anything to them but they might mention it to Dr. Nelson. Just as these thoughts ran through her mind, she heard the door close and footsteps walk away down the hall.

Just as she was pulling herself up, she heard "well hello Dr. Nelson". She dropped back down to the floor. She heard Dr. Fleming and Dr. Nelson talking out in the hall. Oh crap! What was she going to do? She frantically tried to think of some means of escape. Just then, she heard the bathroom door, across the hall, open and close. The door to the office in which she sat did not open. Apparently, it was Dr. Nelson who had gone into the bathroom. Frantically, with hands shaking, she jumped up, closed the HRC directory, and put the computer back in standby mode. She grabbed her purse and dashed out the door. She had the presence of mind to close the door very softly so that Dr. Nelson would not hear it. She collapsed at her desk and breathed a sigh of relief. She did not have the heart, the stomach, or anything else for all this sleuthing. She told herself that, if Dan wanted anything else, he was going to have to get it himself.

Chapter 30

Ben was whistling as he walked back into his office after lunch. He was in a very good mood. Why shouldn't he be? Things were right on track. Both the camera and interface implant devices had recently been delivered from Biotronics, ahead of schedule. The final stages of work getting ready for the implantation procedure were going well. Thanks to Dan's investment, the financial outlook was excellent, and thanks to Dan's work, they should be ready to take the company public immediately following the implantation procedure. Yes sir, everything was going just great. He was thinking about this as he sat down behind his desk.

His eyes landed on the latest progress report from Dr. Fleming concerning some problems that they were trying to sort out having to do with connecting the neural interface to certain parts of the optic nerve. Ben quickly scanned the report and it looked like things were progressing nicely. They almost had the problem solved. This pleased him greatly because the IPO could not occur until the implantation procedure had been done and so there did not need to be any delay.

And while he was thinking about the IPO, he needed to check some reports that Dan had recently sent him concerning preparation for the IPO. He spun around to face his computer. His eyes landed on a light blue penlight lying beside the computer. Strange, he didn't remember leaving that there. Hmmm, perhaps Dr. Fleming had left it there when he had left the report. Dr. Fleming wouldn't have been over here at the computer though. Strange. Oh well, Ben assumed that he had left it there at some point and had just forgotten about it.

He brought the computer out of standby. He opened the directory which contained the financial records, where he had saved the reports from Dan. He was just about to click on the file that he wanted when something caught his eye. There were two items labeled "HRC". Strange. There should be only one directory labeled

"HRC". On farther examination, he found that there was only one directory labeled "HRC" but there was also another "HRC" which was a Zip file. That made no sense, unless he had accidently created the zip file by clicking on the wrong thing or hitting the wrong key at some point. Then, his eyes roamed over to the time/date stamp for the file and his heart rate doubled. The Zip file had been created at 12:27pm today. He looked at his watch. It was now 12:45pm. He had been back at his desk for only perhaps five minutes, ten at the absolute most. This Zip file had been created when he was not in the room. What the heck!

He called Christine and told her to get Zach Harris on the phone. Zach was the owner of the computer company that Vision Biotech used for computer and network maintenance. In just a minute, Christine reported that she had Zach on the line. Ben quickly snatched up the receiver.

"Zach, is there any reason that my computer would spontaneously create a Zip file, while I am not even using the machine?"

"No, not that I can think of. Some backup software might automatically create Zip files but not the backup package that I installed on your network. Why?"

"I have a Zip file here, on my computer, that I didn't create."

"Well, Ben, it shouldn't be a problem. Zip files are just copies of files or directories that are compressed in order to save storage space."

"Yes yes yes, I know that! But, I'm telling you, I didn't create this Zip file and that worries me. I'm trying to figure out where it came from. Remind me, why do people use Zip files?"

"All kinds of reasons. One good reason would be to combine a bunch of files together into a single file in order to make E-mailing easier."

All of the blood drained from Ben' face and he slowly hung up the receiver without responding to Zach. Of course, E-mail, why didn't he think of that. He quickly opened his E-mail program and looked in the "sent items" folder. He found nothing of consequence. Then, he checked the "deleted items" folder. Still nothing. He sat there and drummed his fingers, deep in thought. Then, he had an idea. He picked up the phone and called Christine.

"Hey, Dr. Nelson. What can I do for you?"

"Christine, I hate to ask but could you go down the street and get me a large black coffee? We're working round the clock to get everything ready for the IPO and Jake's implantation procedure and I really need some caffeine."

"Yes sir. Don't we have any coffee in the break room?"

"We do but I bought something different this time and I don't like it."

"OK, sure, be right back."

"Thanks. Come in here and I'll give you the money."

When she came into his office, she had a bit of a concerned look on her face. Ben thought "if what I suspect is true then you have reason to be concerned" but he said nothing as he handed her the money.

After she left, Ben sat down at her desk and opened her E-mail program. Nothing in the inbox. Hmmm. Maybe he was wrong. Better look at the other folders, just to be sure. He looked at the "sent items" folder. There it was. An E-mail to Dan, sent five minutes ago, with a file attachment called "HRC.zip". Well, well, well.

As he got up and headed back into his office, a wave of dread washed over him. He wasn't sure what this development would mean for his future and the future of the company. And he sure was not looking forward to the phone call that he now had to make.

Chapter 31

Vinnie sat in his office, talking to Barry. He had received the call from Ben about an hour before and now he was working on getting something done. His plans had changed somewhat since the last time that he and Barry had discussed the situation.

"So, Vinnie, I thought that you wanted me to beat the crap out of this Dan guy if he stepped out of line. Now, you are telling me that you don't want me to do that but you want for me to rough up a woman and a blind guy instead? That seems a little unfair, even to me. I mean, the woman I can handle, I guess. But, a blind guy? Come on man."

"First of all, I don't want you to beat up the blind guy. I just want you to grab him and bring him to me. Same for the woman. I am going to use them as leverage to get what I want from the accountant. The blind guy is the accountant's brother and the woman is his girlfriend."

"OK, but why not just let me rough up the accountant if he is the one causing the trouble? Why take the roundabout way. The more people who are involved, the bigger chance that something will go wrong."

"Yeah, well, that's the problem. Too many people are involved already. It turns out that Dan has gotten involved with a girl who works for my client. That's the woman who you are going to grab. Her name is Christine. Christine is helping Dan to get information that he shouldn't have. Together, they are in a position to make a lot of trouble for my client. If they do that, then my client can't pay me, and he owes me a whole lot of money. I suspect that Dan's brother, Jake, the blind guy, may know about the situation. Also, Dan's and Jake's father is a big attorney, retired, but still with plenty of pull. If he knows about the situation, he could cause us plenty of trouble. Not to mention that I don't know who Christine may have talked to. Way too many people are involved and we can't rough up or kill everybody."

"What exactly are you going to do?"

"I am going to strike a bargain with Dan. I will trade Jake's sight and Christine's safety for the silence of Dan and anyone else who may know about the situation."

"So, when do you want to do this?"

"Probably in about three months. That is supposed to be when the blind guy has his procedure. If their time table changes, we may have to adjust things a bit, so stay close. Timing is crucial if I am going to have the leverage that I need to force my hand."

"OK, no problem."

Chapter 32

Three months later.

Dan and Christine sat across the table from each other in the cafeteria of the hospital in Memphis.

They had been at the hospital since 5:30 a.m. Jake was supposed to be there for the implantation procedure by 6:00 a.m. He had ridden to Memphis with Dan and Christine had met them there. Gary and Ramona had arrived shortly thereafter. Things had gotten started much faster than Dan and Christine had expected. Jake was checked in by 6:00 and was in his room by 6:30. At 7:00, Dr. Nelson, Fleming, and Crowder had arrived, giving Jake a pep talk and letting him know what to expect. Jake was in the pre-op area by 7:30 and in the OR by 8:00. The surgery was supposed to take about eight hours so, for quite a while, there was nothing to do but sit and wait.

For a while, everyone had talked about the procedure and what it would mean for Jake. He would not come back from surgery with sight. The sight wouldn't happen for a couple weeks yet. The doctors had explained that, today, the artificial retinas and the neural interface devices would be implanted. Then, they would wait about two weeks for everything to start to heal. At the end of the two weeks, if everything was going well, then the implants would be activated, at the Vision Biotech facilities. If everything worked as expected, at that point, for the first time in many years, Jake would see, and he would see better than he had ever seen. Everyone had things to say about what this would mean for Jake and the possibilities that it would open up. Of course, the possibility existed that the technology would not work or that something would go wrong but very little was said about this. After quite a while, they finally managed to wear the subject out.

Then, for a while, Gary read a book, Ramona read some magazines, Christine played with her iPad, and Dan worked on his laptop computer. Finally, about 11:00, Dan closed his laptop and stood. He said "I don't know about the rest of you but I can't sit here anymore". He asked if anyone would like to go get something to eat. Gary and Ramona declined, saying that they might stretch their legs a little but that they would prefer to remain near the room in case Dr. Nelson called. Christine said that she would love to get something and she and Dan set off in search of the cafeteria.

They were very happy for Jake but the subject of Jake and the procedure had already been talked to death so, now that they were alone, they wanted to discuss other matters.

"Once the procedure is done, are you going to take action concerning the dirty money?"

"Yes, I think I have to. I hate to do it, for several reasons, not least of which is that I will lose a lot of money, but I can't just stand by and let an IPO go through when I know that much of the company's accomplishments have been funded with dirty money and that the company will be used to launder that money. I am the CFO and an investor. If someone gets wind of what's going on, I would never be able to work as a CPA again. Not to mention the possible jail time."

Christine laughed.

"Oh, it would be OK. I'd visit you in jail."

Dan laughed too.

"Not much consolation, I'm afraid."

"I don't know why I'm joking about this. The situation scares me to death. I helped you to get the records that will expose them. As far as I know, they don't know that but they will have to find out, at some point. I don't imagine they will be happy about that."

"No, they won't. Those documents had Vinnie Patrillo's name all over them. As soon as I saw those files, I knew what I had to do and I knew that you and I would both be in great danger. I got you into this mess and I need to find a way to protect you."

"You didn't get me into anything. As I recall, you didn't want for me to have anything to do with this. I insisted. I got myself into this."

"Well, still."

His words trailed off and they sat in silence for several minutes. When he spoke again, he sounded a little nervous.

"One thing is for sure. It would be much easier to protect you if you were with me all of the time."

She smiled.

"I wish I could be."

"You can be, if you want to be."

He reached into his pocket and pulled out a ring. The diamond wasn't the biggest that she had ever seen but it was the prettiest.

"This may not be the most romantic setting but I just can't wait for a better one. I am no good at romantic speeches so I'm not going to try. Christine Dunning, will you marry me?"

Christine looked stunned and, for a second, Dan was worried. Then, tears slowly filled her eyes. She jumped up and ran around to his side of the table and, before he could stand, she grabbed him and squeezed him so tightly that he could hardly breathe. Through her tears, she spoke.

"Yes, yes, yes, I will marry you."

At hearing this, to his surprise, Dan started to cry too. They made quite a sight, holding on to each other, crying, in the middle of the hospital cafeteria. After they disengaged, they sat there and talked over a few of the details. They wanted to get married quickly. Also, both of them had big weddings, the first time, and had no desire to repeat that. They were both happier than they could ever remember being and they ended up sitting there, talking, for most of the afternoon.

Finally, they went back to Jake's room, to wait for news of the surgery and to tell Gary and Ramona the good news.

Chapter 33

Two weeks later.

Jake sat in his study and contemplated the days ahead. Tomorrow, his implants would be activated and, hopefully, he would see. His eyes were healing nicely from the surgical procedure to implant the devices two weeks previous and almost all of the discomfort that he had originally felt was gone. He was absolutely ecstatic at the prospect of having close to normal vision. Of course, he knew that there was a chance that it wouldn't work but he couldn't let himself think about that. He knew that, for a while after the implants were activated, he would not be able to concentrate on work and so he thought that he had better try to get some work done now. He thought "well, better get the day started".

He checked his E-mail and found nothing of consequence. He then opened the directory which contained his novel in progress. He opened the latest chapter and used the screen reader to read what he had written yesterday. He liked it, though there were a couple of minor changes that he wanted to make. He could now smell the coffee brewing and he decided that he would make the changes after getting his first cup.

As he was about to pass out of the study, he subconsciously raised his left hand and touched the light switch, just to the left of the door. He froze. The switch was in the up position, which meant that the light was on. Being completely blind in both eyes, lacking even light perception, he did not use the lights when no one else was in the house. He tried to remember the last time that someone had been here, in the study, when the lights would have been on. Two or three days previous, Dan had been here. They had sat in the study and discussed the activation of Jake's implants. Had the light remained on when Dan had left and been on ever since? Jake didn't know but he was beginning to get the creeps again.

He went down the hall to the kitchen. By feel, he located a cup in the cabinet above the coffee maker and pored himself a cup. He stood there for a second, sipping the coffee, hoping that the hot liquid would help to dispel the chill that was beginning to settle over him. Had that light been on since Dan left? He just didn't know. It was on now. If Dan had not left it on, what did that mean? Should he call Dan and ask if he had turned it off?

He pulled his iPhone out of his pocket and pressed the home button. It announced 4:53. Was Dan up? Probably so, he was an early riser. He unlocked the phone, opened the phone app, and found Dan's name in the list of favorite contacts. He paused before double tapping in order to place the call. Even if Dan was up, which was not a certainty, he probably wouldn't remember whether or not he had turned the light off. People just didn't remember things like that, especially two days later. He locked the phone and put it back in his pocket. Then, he grabbed his coffee and headed back for the study.

As he came into the study, he turned the light off. He sat down again in front of his computer. He decided to read the last page again in order to decide exactly how to make the changes that he wanted to make. As he reached for the keyboard, he felt a small circle of steel pressed against the base of his neck. A voice from behind him and just to his left said "that looks like a pretty good book that you are writing and if you want to live to finish it, do not move".

Jake's heart froze.

"What you feel on your neck is the barrel of a gun."

"I figured that much out myself."

"Don't get smart. I am going to step back. Don't try anything."

The cold steel left Jake's neck and he felt a little better about the situation, but not much.

"OK, stand up."

Jake stood, very shakily.

"Walk to the door that goes out into the garage. Go slow."

Jake did as he was told. Even though he was walking slowly, he kept bumping into things. He was so nervous that he couldn't concentrate enough to keep his bearings. When they finally reached the door, the voice said "take two steps out into the garage and stop". Jake did so. In a few seconds, he heard the door close and he felt a hand roughly push him from behind. The hand half pushed, half guided him to a spot on the other side of the garage. He heard a car door open and the voice said "get in". Jake had to feel around a little to figure out how to accomplish this because he didn't know what kind of vehicle that it was and he didn't know how he was oriented in relation to it. He pretty quickly determined that it was a sedan of some sort and he got in with no trouble. The car door slammed and he sat in silence for a few seconds until he heard the driver's door open and close. Then, he heard the voice, from the driver's seat.

"OK, this is what is going to happen. We are going to go for a little ride. That's all it is, a ride. I am not going to hurt you, as long as you don't do something to make me. Don't make any sudden moves and don't do anything to draw attention to us. Do you understand?"

Jake nodded.

They backed out of the garage and pulled onto the street.

Chapter 34

When Christine arrived at work, there were two cars in the parking lot that she did not recognize, both of them with Illinois plates. She didn't think too much of it. The company was planning to go public shortly. There had been a lot of activity around the place lately, related to the upcoming IPO, and she assumed that these unfamiliar vehicles had something to do with that.

When she came into the reception area, there was a man who she did not know sitting at her desk. He was on the short side of medium height, a bit over weight, dark complected, with short black hair. She paused for a moment, trying to place him, but she could not. As she approached the desk, he stood and extended his hand.

"Hello Ms. Dunning, I believe that you know me or, at least, know of me. My name is Vinnie Petrillo."

Christine's heart rate doubled. If Vinnie Petrillo was here and if he knew that she knew of him, this could not be good. She turned to leave and a large man, who she had not noticed before, stepped in front of the door, blocking her path.

"Ms. Dunning, why are you in such a hurry to leave? You just got here. Stay for a while. Come sit down in the break room and get comfortable."

She silently and franticly prayed "Lord, these are mobsters, they may be killers, please please protect me".

"Why do you want me to stay?"

"We just want to talk to you."

"OK, we can talk right here."

"We don't want to talk just yet. Your boyfriend will be joining us in a little while. We want to talk to him too. It will be easier to just wait and talk to everyone at once."

Her dread deepened.

"Dan? He is coming?"

"Oh yes, he is coming and His brother is here too."

"Jake is here? But why?"

"So many questions. And we will answer all of them but not until everyone is here. You are going to have to wait a while. Now, just come on back here and get comfortable."

Chapter 35

Dan sat at his desk, deep in thought. The last week had been one of the happiest of his life. The woman of his dreams was going to marry him and his blind brother was probably about to have almost as good eye site as Dan had. Then, there was this darned mess with Vision biotech. Dan was probably about to lose a couple million and his whole family was going to have to constantly look over their shoulders for the Patrillos. He was both extraordinarily happy and extraordinarily apprehensive, a strange mix of emotions.

Dan's cell phone rang. He looked at the caller ID. It was Vision Biotech. Darn, he didn't really want to talk to them right now. No doubt, it was Ben, with yet another problem regarding the IPO. OH well, he thought, better go ahead and deal with whatever it is. After all, he was the CFO and part owner, for now anyway. He answered the phone.

"Hello."

"Hi Dan, how are you doing this fine morning."

Strange, Dan didn't recognize the voice. Perhaps he had misread the caller ID. Well, whoever it was knew his name so they must have the right number.

"I'm just fine. With whom am I speaking?"

"Oh, I'm sorry. It was terribly rude of me not to introduce myself. This is Vinnie Petrillo."

Oh crap, Vinnie Petrillo. Dan hadn't expected to actually talk to the man. Not yet anyway. He was a bit puzzled as to what this little development might mean. Apparently it showed in his voice when he answered.

"Mr. Petrillo, what can I do for you today?"

"Dan, you sound a little surprised to hear from me. Do you know who I am?"

"Well, I have heard of you."

Vinnie laughed.

"Don't believe everything that you hear. I am not nearly as bad as people say. I don't think that your girlfriend likes me though."

Dan was a bit taken aback but he tried not to panic. Of course, if Vinnie was at the Vision Biotech facility, then he would have seen Christine. This didn't necessarily mean anything. Still, Dan was a bit unsettled.

"Oh, I'm sure that she likes you fine. Perhaps she is just having a bad day."

"Yes, I think that she would agree that she is having a bad day. If you were to ask her, I bet she would even blame me."

Dan's unease went up a notch but he said nothing. He couldn't think of anything to say. After a slight pause, Vinnie spoke again.

"I don't think that your brother likes me either."

Now, Dan's unease went up about ten notches and he couldn't hold back the panic any more. If Jake was being brought into the conversation, this had to be very bad. He tried and failed to keep the panic out of his voice.

"What does Jake have to do with anything?"

"How about you and I discuss that face to face? We are all waiting on you, me, Christine, Jake. The party can't start until you get here so come on. You are the only other invited guest. If you bring

222

anyone else, I will be very unhappy. If I get unhappy then a lot of other people will be unhappy too. Do you understand me?"

Dan's heart rate doubled, he started sweating, and a wave of intense nausea swept over him. He had to get himself under control. He wasn't going to do Christine and Jake any good if he had a heart attack right here.

"Dan? Are you there?"

Dan stammered when he spoke.

"Yes sir, I understand you perfectly. I'm on my way."

"Excellent. We are all waiting."

Dan had stood during the conversation and begun pacing. When he hung up, he collapsed into his chair. Obviously, Vinnie knew that Dan knew about him. Obviously, he was going to trade Christine and Jake for Dan's silence. Well, maybe not. He might hurt one or both of them, just to prove to Dan that he was willing to do whatever was necessary to protect his money. Or, for that matter, he might just kill all of them. What in the world was Dan supposed to do? His mind was racing as he buried his face in his hands.

Two things were certain. He could not let Christine and Jake get hurt however he had to prevent it. And he wasn't going to accomplish anything just sitting there. He jumped up, grabbed his keys, and ran out the door.

Chapter 36

Jake sat in the patient's chair, in the exam room, at Vision Biotech. As soon as he had arrived, he had been brought in here. The man who had brought him, Jake thought his name was Barry, had wanted to stay and keep an eye on him. The man called Vinnie, who seemed to be the one in charge, wanted Barry to go and take care of something else. Jake had heard Vinnie whisper "go on, what's he going to do, he's blind". For once, Jake was glad that someone didn't take him seriously because of his blindness. Now, if he could only come up with a way to use that to his advantage.

Jake could hear voices coming through the wall on his left. He thought that the break room would be over there but he wasn't positive because he just hadn't paid that much attention to the layout of the building. He had always been with Dan, on the few occasions that he had been here previously, and so he hadn't had to memorize the layout of the building in order to get around. Through the wall, he couldn't understand what was being said but he could hear the voices clearly enough to identify them. He had heard Vinnie's voice and he was pretty sure that, at one point, he had heard Christine's voice. He hadn't heard Barry's voice but Jake was pretty sure that he would be somewhere else, taking care of whatever Vinnie had wanted.

Jake sat and thought about his surroundings. Having been in the room before, he knew that it was small, perhaps only seven or eight feet by ten or twelve feet. He knew that the slit lamp, a device used to examine the eye, was mounted on an articulation arm to his left and could be swung out in front of him. He placed his hand out in front of him and felt nothing, as he had expected. The slit lamp would be positioned to the left, out of the way, as there was no eye exam currently going on.

He knew that, across the room, directly in front of him, there was a desk where the doctor wrote notes in the chart. He could hear what sounded like a small fan, coming from about where he knew the desk to be. He assumed that it was probably a computer. He wanted to get to it because, if it was a computer, he could use it to send a message for help, if he could find a way to operate it. He couldn't see the screen and it wouldn't have his speech software on it. Well, he thought, one thing at a time. First, to find it.

He stood, careful not to trip on the foot rest of the exam chair, and took a tentative step forward. He bumped the stool on which the doctor sat during an exam. It had wheels and he pushed it aside. He felt out in front of him and took a couple more tentative steps until his hand touched the wooden edge of the desk. He trailed his hand along the side of the desk as he went around to the other side. He reached out, found the chair, and sat down.

He reached out In front of him, with both hands, and slowly and gently felt around. To his right, he touched what appeared to be the front edge of a laptop computer. As he felt around it more, he felt the keyboard and screen. He kept feeling around on it, exploring the contours of the computer. He wanted to locate USB ports, card slots, and such. He really wasn't sure why though. If only he had a flash drive with JAWS on it. Wait, what was that he was feeling? Under his left index finger, he felt the little apple with a bite out of it. This was the Apple logo.

Apparently, this was a Mac. Jake was excited. This was good news. All Apple products came with Voice Over built in, which is the same speech software that his iPhone used. This was terrific. It didn't matter that he didn't have a copy of JAWS with him. He had a screen reader, right here, built in.

There was a small problem though. Although Jake used Voice Over on his iPhone all of the time, it didn't work in exactly the same way on a Mac that it did on an iPhone. Normally, this wouldn't be a problem. He would just read a few things on the internet and listen to a few podcasts and figure it out. However, he didn't usually have guys, who were very unhappy with him for some reason and who probably had guns, in the next room. Jake thought that this would probably hamper his efforts. He didn't think that a request for his iPhone back so that he could listen to some podcasts on how to operate this computer would be met with much enthusiasm. He was going to have to think of something else.

At one time, not long ago, Jake had thought about getting a Mac. At that time, he had listened to a few podcasts concerning how to operate Voice Over on a Mac. He sat and pondered and tried to remember how to turn Voice Over on. He figured that, if he could just do that, he could figure out the rest. Suddenly, it hit him, the key combination to turn on Voice Over was command F5. The keyboard wasn't exactly like what he was used to. He couldn't remember for sure which key was command but he knew that it was just to the left of the space bar. He tried the first key to the left of the space bar and, sure enough, that was it. As soon as he pressed the keys, Voice Over came on alright, and it very loudly announced its presence. Apparently the computer was turned up to full volume. In a voice that practically rattled the instruments on the shelves, a male voice said "Voice Over on".

Jake got to his feet just in time to hear Vinnie's voice, from next door, say "what the heck". Jake banged his knee on the desk, half tripped on the doctor's stool, and just barely made it into the exam chair, just as Vinnie came in.

"What was that sound in here?"

"Sound, what sound?"

"It sounded like someone yelled in here."

"No one yelled in here."

"Are you sure?"

"Pretty sure. I can't see but I can hear fine."

"Don't get smart."

"Sorry."

"Then what was that noise?"

"What noise?"

"I told you, it sounded like someone yelled in here."

"And I told you, no one yelled in here. We already covered this."

Jake was praying that the computer wouldn't pick now to yell something about the latest update. Vinnie would probably reflexively shoot the computer and then shoot Jake. He figured that he had better come up with something.

"Um, I sneezed."

"Didn't sound like a sneeze."

"It was a very big sneeze. There's probably snot everywhere so watch your step."

"Look, blind or not, you had better quit getting smart with me."

"Yes sir."

"And be quiet in here."

"Yes sir."

Jake heard the door close.

He breathed a sigh of relief as he got up and made his way back to the desk. Hmmm, how to turn the volume down. He thought that he could figure out Voice Over just by playing around with it but not if it was yelling at him. He didn't think that he could convince Vinnie that he was sneezing that much. What about ear phones? If he had on ear phones, his ear drums might bust before he got the volume figured out but at least some other and more vital part of him might not get busted by Vinnie. He searched through the drawers in the tiny desk. In the last one, under a pile of junk, he found an iPod with ear buds. Thank goodness. He felt around the side of the computer until he found the earphone slot and plugged in the ear buds. The first key that he pressed made his ears ring and he figured that he had better figure out the volume fast. With this thing yelling in his ears, he wouldn't hear Vinnie or the other guy coming.

Fortunately, though Voice Over on the Mac wasn't the same as Voice Over on his iPhone, there were similarities and he had the basics figured out pretty quickly. He was going through the home screen, looking for the mail program. He planned to send a message to his Dad and just hope that he would see it quickly. It was all that he could think of to do. Then, he came across a program that caught his attention. It was called "VBT Interface". Hmmm, what was this? He ran the program.

He was presented with a screen that was full of information and options, all of which seemed to relate to his recently implanted devices. He was astounded. They had said that the implants were controlled through a wireless Bluetooth interface. Apparently, this was the program that was used for that. This was absolutely fantastic. If he could figure this out, he could activate his implants. Then, wouldn't Vinnie and the others be in for a surprise? He had to figure it out first though.

He examined the various screens and options. He supposed that first, he would need to activate the neural interface devices. Without them, the artificial retinas wouldn't do any good because the signals wouldn't go anywhere. In the list of devices that could be activated or deactivated, the left neural interface was the first one in the list. Jake thought "well, may as well start with that one" and he clicked on it.

Chapter 37

Dan's hands were shaking on the steering wheel as he glanced at the speedometer. The indicator was just passing 90. He looked back at I-40. He couldn't believe the situation that he was in. He was about to marry the girl of his dreams and Jake was about to receive near perfect eyesight. Now, he was on his way to, hopefully, rescue them both from some sort of mob crime boss. And what the heck was he supposed to do when he got there? He was an accountant. He knew nothing about how to handle situations like this.

His thoughts were interrupted by his cell phone ringing. It was Vinnie.

"Hey Dan. Are you on your way?"

"Of course I am."

"OK, just wanted to make sure. I'm about to get tired of your brother's smart mouth. I hope that nothing happens to him before you get here."

"You leave Jake alone!"

"Oh, I have, so far. Lucky for him that he's blind. If not for that, I would have had his face rearranged already. Of course, the plan is to take care of the whole blindness thing, right? I hope that can still happen."

"I would love for him to be able to see but, right now, my only concern is his safety."

"Oh, you can rest assured that we won't kill him. I need him. He is the first clinical trial patient. If he doesn't gain his eyesight, then Vision Biotech doesn't stand a chance and I will never see a dime of my money."

"That is what this is all about isn't it? The money."

"Oh yes, of course it is. We can discuss the situation when you get here. And step on it. I said that we won't kill him but I didn't say that he will remain in pristine condition."

"What about Christine?"

"Well, unlike Jake, we don't really need her. However, I don't like to perpetrate violence just for the sake of doing it so, if you do as I ask, she should be fine. It would be a shame for that pretty face to get messed up."

"You scum bucket!"

"Thank you. See you shortly. Like I said, step on it. Oh yes, and remember to come alone."

He hung up.

Dan pressed down harder on the accelerator and desperately tried to think of what he should do.

Chapter 38

Jake was just about to click on the link to activate the left neural interface when he heard a noise out in the hall which caused him to jump. This caused him to click on the link for the right interface instead. Immediately, he perceived a greenish flash and he was hit with a wave of dizziness. The dizziness quickly subsided. He guessed it was his brain getting use to the new signal. The noise in the hall continued, which made him very nervous. No time to activate the left interface. Where was the link to activate the right artificial retina? His unfamiliarity with the computer along with his nervousness combined to make the task very difficult. Finally, he located the link and clicked it.

The dizziness that he had previously experienced was nothing compared to this. He tried to stand but got only half way up before he fell. He fell behind the desk and, as he did so, the chair, which was on wheels, rolled out of the way. He reflexively squeezed his eyes shut and clutched the side of the desk. The room was spinning violently and, for a second, he thought that he might vomit. Gradually, the dizziness and nausea started to subside.

Jake heard the door open. He could now hear the noises, which were coming from the hall, more clearly. He could hear Christine yelling "let go of me" and he could hear Barry's voice angrily saying "get back in there". Apparently, Christine had tried to run but hadn't gotten far.

He also heard Vinnie, just inside the door, saying "what the heck, where did he go". He then heard Vinnie yelled "he's gone, find him". At first, this puzzled Jake. Then, he understood. He had fallen behind the desk, which was across the room from the door, and so, from the door, Vinnie wouldn't be able to see him. He could now hear Vinnie talking again but it now sounded like he was down the hall. Jake figured that Vinnie would be back soon and he had to figure out what to do before he came back.

OK, time to test the implants. He was still squeezing his eyes shut. He slowly opened them. He was immediately slightly disoriented. He hadn't seen anything at all in 20 years and, even then, not in nearly this much detail. He was also slightly dizzy but nothing like before. He could deal with it. The implants were working alright but he didn't have time to enjoy the experience.

At first, what he saw confused him. A little black rectangle on a light colored background. He reached out and touched it, to get a sense of it in the way that he was used to, by feel. It was an electrical outlet. He had forgotten that he was sitting on the floor, facing a wall. He could see but he hadn't even recognized an electrical outlet. He was going to have to do better if he was to use this sudden advantage that he had found to help to save Christine and get them both out of here. As he shakily got to his feet, he tried to think back to when he previously had a little vision. It had been nothing like this but perhaps he could use it as a reference to help him to recognize and understand the things that he now saw.

He turned and surveyed the room. At first, as he turned, the dizziness increased again and he grabbed the corner of the desk to steady himself but then it quickly subsided. He looked around the room for something that he could use for a weapon. This process was much slower than he would have liked. First of all, there wasn't much in the room that could be used as a weapon. After all, this was just a room for doing eye exams. Second, he had to slowly work to correctly interpret everything that he saw. It was getting better though. OK, no decent weapons. What was he supposed to do now? Club Vinnie over the head with a MacBook?

Then, he saw it, on the floor, sticking out slightly from behind the exam chair. He wasn't sure what it was. He could only see an inch or two of it. What he could see was cylindrical. It appeared to be a handle of some sort. He slowly walked up to the exam chair and looked behind it, holding onto the chair for support because he still had a little intermittent dizziness. Behind the chair, he saw, well, he wasn't sure what he saw. What was it? He still wasn't 100% effective at correctly interpreting the visual input that he was getting. He knelt down and felt of the object. It was a large socket wrench. He supposed that it had been used in the installation of the exam chair or other equipment and had been accidently left here. It wasn't as good as something like a shotgun but it was large and relatively heavy. It would make a good club.

He could hear Vinnie arguing with Christine now.

"Where is Jake?"

"I told you, I don't know. I haven't seen him in several days."

"He didn't talk to you after he escaped?"

"Now how in the heck could he talk to me? You have been in here almost the whole time. I didn't even know that Jake had escaped until you just came in here, ranting about it."

Jake slowly proceeded down the hall, toward the voices, which were coming from the open break room door, which was just ahead, on his right. He clutched the socket wrench in his right hand. Vinnie was yelling louder now.

"You know something, you have a smart mouth. Almost as smart as Jake's. It's going to get both of you in trouble."

Jake stepped into the doorway. Vinnie's back was facing him. Jake figured that it was now or never. Jake raised the socket wrench. When he did so, Christine, who was facing Vinnie, saw him. She couldn't suppress the look of surprise on her face. Vinnie saw her expression change as she glanced behind him. Vinnie turned to look behind him as the socket wrench was in the middle of its arch toward his head. It was too late for him to do anything to stop it. Jake felt the impact through the handle of the wrench and heard a sickening crunch sound as the end of the wrench made contact with Vinnie's nose. Vinnie let out a sudden yelp of pain as his hands flew to his ruined nose, from which blood pored. Vinnie was momentarily paralyzed by the pain and the shock of seeing Jake standing there. Jake took the opportunity to deliver a vicious kick to Vinnie's crotch. Vinnie let out an earsplitting howl of pain and collapsed to the floor.

After Vinnie fell, Jake could see Christine clearly. He immediately noticed two things. First, she was even more beautiful than he had imagined. Second, she had a gun in her hand which was pointed at Vinnie. After a moment in which Jake and Christine both sized up the situation and Vinnie just lay there groaning, Jake spoke.

"Hey, good to see you, literally."

"You mean?"

"Yes, I can see, out of my right eye anyway. I managed to activate the implants on that side."

"Congratulations."

"Thanks. We can celebrate later. What do we need to do?"

"I'm sure that he has a gun. Get it."

Jake knelt and felt of Vinnie's jacket. Sure enough, there was a bulge on the left side, which proved to be a shoulder holster. Jake withdrew a large, black handgun from the holster and handed it to Christine.

As he did so, he said "where is Barry". He heard a voice from behind him say "right here", as he received a blow that knocked him over Vinnie's body, into Christine. Both Jake and Christine fell into a heap on the floor. When they looked up, Barry was standing over them, holding a gun that looked like the one that Jake had just taken from Vinnie. When Jake had fell into Christine, Vinnie's gun had gone flying out of his hand and it now lay on the floor next to Barry's foot. Barry slowly knelt and picked it up, placing it in his own shoulder holster, never taking his eyes or his gun sites from Christine and Jake. As he stood, he spoke.

"Well, until I heard Vinnie in here yelling, I was out there waiting for Dan. We were all just going to sit down and have a nice little talk. However, now, I don't think that our little talk will be quite so nice. First of all, Christine, hand over that other gun."

"What other gun?"

"Don't play games with me. Give me the gun, right now. Slide it over here."

"Very reluctantly, she placed the gun on the tile floor and gave it a hard shove in Barry's direction."

He knelt and retrieved it, still not taking his own gun sites from Christine and Jake.

"Now, get up, slowly."

They did as they were told.

"Now, each of you, take a chair."

They did so.

Barry pulled a large role of duct tape from his pocket.

Jake couldn't resist.

"Well, quite a well prepared thug, aren't you?"

"Shut up!"

Barry bound them both, hands and feet, and secured them to their chairs. Almost as an afterthought, he taped their mouths. Then, he spoke to Vinnie.

"I'm sorry to leave you there but I have to go and wait for Dan. We can't have him managing to surprise us. Don't worry, they will pay for this."

Chapter 39

Dan pulled into the parking lot at Vision Biotech and saw three vehicles, Christine's Explorer and two sedans with Illinois plates. Well, that was just great. Apparently, Vinnie had brought some extra muscle with him.

He quickly parked and then sat there pondering the situation. He did own a gun but it was back at his parents' house. He hadn't taken the time to go by and get it, a decision for which he now chastised himself. Christine and Jake were in there with Vinnie and no telling who else. No doubt, they were armed. Vinnie had said that they just wanted to talk but Dan knew that was unlikely. He quickly looked around the interior of the truck, searching for a possible weapon. He found nothing. Well, nothing to do but go and see what awaits. He got out of the truck and a feeling of increasing dread descended on him as he walked across the parking lot.

As he entered the reception area, everything was as it had been on the last occasion that he had been there, accept that the area was now empty. He heard voices coming from the door behind Christine's desk, which led to the main hallway. As he passed by the desk, he looked for a weapon, but he saw nothing more deadly than a stapler.

As he proceeded into the hallway, he could tell that the voices were coming from the door on his left and just ahead, the middle of three doors, the break room. He stopped, just inches from the door jamb, and listened.

"OK, in just a second, I'm going to go out there and wait for Dan. I hate to leave you like this, well, no I don't. If you had behaved yourself, this wouldn't have been necessary."

Dan didn't recognize the voice that was speaking. He had never heard it before. Probably some of Vinnie's muscle. As the man continued to talk, Dan very slowly backed up to the bathroom door, which was the first door in the hall. He slowly turned the knob and very slowly eased the door open, praying that the hinges wouldn't squeak. He eased into the bathroom and very quietly shut the door. He could hear the man's voice coming through the wall. He now had the advantage that he was in the building but without them knowing it yet. He knew that the man would have to pass by here on his way out front to wait for Dan and Dan hoped that the guy wouldn't have to use the bathroom. Dan would wait for him to pass by and then he would sneak over into the break room, presumably where Christine and Jake were, and, together, they would figure out what to do.

Dan couldn't understand the man's words through the wall but he could hear him clearly enough to know when he stopped speaking. Just a few seconds later, Dan heard his footsteps pass by and he heard the door, at the end of the hall, open and then close. Dan stood there for a couple minutes, to make sure that he wasn't coming back, and then Dan eased out into the hall and down to the break room.

He found Jake and Christine, sitting at the table, each of them with their hands and feet bound and with a strip of tape over their mouth. On the floor was a man that Dan didn't recognize, who was moving little but moaning a lot. Dan stepped over the man in the floor and quickly cut Jake's and Christine's bindings, with his pocket knife, and removed the tape from their mouths. As Dan hugged Christine, he spoke to Jake.

"Who is this guy on the floor?"

"That's Vinnie Petrillo. I clobbered him with a socket wrench and kicked him in the crotch."

"Remind me not to call you a nerd again. Who is the guy who just left here?"

"That's Barry somebody. He's the guy who kidnapped me this morning. He went out there to wait for you."

"Yeah, I heard."

"Won't he be surprised to find that you're already here?"

"I certainly hope so."

"Oh, by the way, you need a shave."

"Well I, wait a minute, how do you know that?"

Christine spoke.

"Einstein here managed to activate the implants in his right eye, which I admit is very very cool, but we need to celebrate later. How are we going to handle Barry when he comes back in here?"

"I don't suppose that you have your gun in your purse?"

"Well, actually, I did have it. The idiots didn't think to check to see if I was carrying. However, I pulled the gun when Jake clobbered Vinnie here so that he could disarm him and Barry snuck up and kind of screwed things up."

"Oh crap. That's too bad."

"Yeah, I have an idea though."

"I'm listening."

Five minutes later, Dan and Jake were stationed inside the bathroom. Jake was holding the door knob, leaning against the door, listening to the sounds in the hall. He was the one by the door because his hearing was more finely tuned. Dan was pressed against Jake's back, ready to lend his muscle to the effort. Jake could hear the sounds from the break room, as they wafted down the hall. Jake

241

heard Christine say "believe it or not, I'm really sorry about this", he heard the crunch of bone as Christine's high heel came down on Vinnie's hand, and he heard Vinnie's blood curdling scream, which brought Barry running. To Dan, Jake said "wait, wait, wait, now". Jake turned the knob and Jake and Dan, simultaneously, put all of their strength and weight against the door. The door flew open and almost tore off it's hinges, just as Barry entered the hall at a dead run. Jake and Dan felt Barry meet the door. There was a huge "thunk" which resounded through Jake's and Dan's bones. Dan said "that even hurt me, I'm sure it hurt you and he's probably darned near dead".

The three of them went to inspect the damage. Barry had been propelled backward so hard that he had hit the reception desk, flipped backward over it, and hit the floor on his head. He lay there, sprawled on the floor, knocked out cold. Like Vinnie, it appeared that Barry also had a broken nose. They hoped that he didn't also have a broken neck. They wanted to neutralize him but certainly not to kill him.

Christine was the first to speak.

"Do you think he's OK?"

Dan said "I think so. He's breathing anyway".

Jake and Christine both let out a sigh of relief.

Jake said "looks like that worked out well".

Christine said "His buddy back there isn't going to be any trouble either".

Dan said "why are you so sure".

Christine said "after I stepped on his hand, I gave him another kick in the crotch, just for good measure".

Dan shook his head.

"I am going to be very careful what I say to both of you from now on."

Christine smiled.

"Nah, the two of you don't have anything to worry about. But those that would hurt you do."

Jake said "brother, I think that you finally found a good one".

Christine laughed.

"You might have something to worry about after all if you don't stop talking about me like an object, as though I wasn't standing right here. Now, Einstein, go call 911."

"OK, OK, I'm going."

Chapter 40

One week later.

Dan and Christine stood in Gary's and Ramona's living room and repeated after the pastor. They had chosen a very small, very simple ceremony. Dan, though not usually an overly emotional man, had tears in his eyes as he repeated his wedding vows, as did Christine. After Dan kissed the bride, he said "you are the most beautiful woman in the world". Jake said "I agree but I haven't seen that many women yet". Christine smiled and punched him on the arm.

"Ever the comedian, aren't you, Einstein?"

"I certainly try."

The only people in attendance were Gary, Ramona, Jake, and Christine's parents. After the five minute ceremony, everyone gathered in the kitchen for refreshments and conversation.

"Well, Jake, looks like everything has turned out just great for the both of us lately."

"Yes, it sure does."

"You are really lucky that you figured out what was going on with that left neural implant before you activated it."

Christine walked up.

"Yeah, leave it to Einstein here to get so curious about how the thing works that he goes exploring all the settings before even turning it on."

"Yeah, well, good thing that it had that little warning posted about voltage exceeding safety limits or whatever it said. I'm going to have to thank the programmer for putting that in there."

"While you're at it, thank him for putting in the feature that keeps records of all computers that access it. Without that, we would have never known that it was James who sabotaged it."

"We still don't know who hired James."

"Yes and we probably won't find out. He has admitted that he was paid to do it and I suspect that he is being paid even more not to say who hired him. Vinnie says that it wasn't him and I don't think that it was. After all, Vinnie had a vested interest in Vision Biotech making it. That's why he was willing to go to such lengths to keep us quiet."

"Speaking of Vinnie, the prosecutor says that Vinnie and Barry are going away for a while. Ironically, they haven't been able to get them on other charges but now they're getting them for kidnapping, along with a few other charges."

"What about Ben?"

"Well, they're going easy on him because he wasn't involved in the kidnapping. He says that he didn't know that it was going to happen. I suspect that he did but that can't be proven. There is also no proof that he knew that the money from the Petrillo Organization was dirty so there's nothing that can be done about that either. However, an IPO of a company, with Ben at the helm, will never go anywhere. Not after all of the bad press that has been generated by the involvement of the Patrillos. Plus, there's the issue of the dirty money having been invested in the company. So, he may not be going to jail but he can say goodbye to his dream of being one of the world's wealthiest people."

"When Ben thought that they were going to prosecute him, he spilled his guts. I couldn't believe that Cathy was involved. She can forget about her dreams of wealth too. I hope that she and Ben are very happy together, though I suspect that, without Ben having either wealth or the prospect of it, she will be gone very shortly."

"What about Vision Biotech? It would be a shame for all the work that has been done to just fall by the wayside."

"That isn't going to happen. A company has been formed, called JDC Biotech, that is going to raise some venture capital and then purchase the patents on the technology from Vision Biotech. With those patents in hand, JDC Biotech will then do what Vision Biotech had planned to do."

"What does JDC stand for?"

"Glad you asked. It stands for Jake, Dan, and Christine."

Chapter 41

"Come on, come on, we're going to be late."

"I'm coming, I'm coming. I'm almost done with my make-up. You never hurried me up like this when we were dating."

"We never had a plane to catch when we were dating."

Dan and Christine were in their room at the Holiday Inn, about to leave for their honeymoon in Hawaii. They hadn't wanted to spend their first night as a married couple in the room where Dan was staying at his parents' house. Neither had they wanted to drive all the way back to Memphis to stay at Christine's apartment. So, after a great afternoon of cake and punch and laughter with their families, they had gotten this room and had a great evening as well. Now, the next morning, their flight was leaving from Memphis at 11:30 and it was now 8:30. Dan was starting to get impatient.

"Maybe we should have stayed at your apartment after all. At least then we would already be in Memphis."

She came and kissed him and then sat down beside him on the bed, a make-up brush in her hand and a mischievous grin on her face.

"now, Dan, would you have really wanted to drive over an hour to my apartment? That could have been a very long hour."

Dan's anxiety about the possibility of missing the flight eased. He got a mischievous grin of his own and he laughed.

"Yeah, I guess you're right."

"Of course I'm right. Now, relax, I'll just be about five more minutes."

She got up and went back into the bathroom and continued talking to him from there.

"I really liked Brother Luke. I think I'd like to visit his church."

Luke Stanley had performed the wedding ceremony and was the pastor of Emmanuel Baptist Church, there in Jackson. They had been looking for someone to do it and Luke was recommended by Christine's pastor in Memphis. This had been fine with Dan, who had never gone to Church with any regularity and who didn't really care who did it, especially given the very simple and short ceremony. Dan had liked Luke just fine and thought that he had done a fine job with the wedding but he wasn't sure about attending his church, or any other church, on a regular basis. Dan didn't say that though. He knew that God was very important to Christine and Dan didn't want her to think that he was belittling that or didn't take it seriously. He just said "yeah, sure, we can do that some time".

Christine said "you don't sound too excited about it" but she was too excited to dwell on one subject for long and before Dan could reply, she said "I think it's great that you're starting JDC Biotech."

Finally, a subject that Dan was more comfortable with.

"Yeah, isn't it cool?"

"It sure is cool. How are you going to get Ben to sell you the rights to the technology?"

"Oh, he already agreed to and we've agreed on a price. I don't really know why he's selling it to me when he could probably get more from another biotech company but I'm not going to question it."

"Well, it sure is very cool and I'm very excited but, I'll be honest, I'm a little uneasy too. I'm not sure why but I am."

"Oh, come on babe, what could possibly go wrong?"

Though he didn't yet know it, that statement would come back to haunt him, very soon.

Note From Author

Hello. I am Scott Duck, the author of "In Full View". I really hope that you enjoyed it and I invite you to visit www.scottduck.com for information about the sequel. Now, if I may, I would like to take a moment to talk with you about the most important thing in my life.

In the book, the character of Jake is blind and, as a result, he faces some rather unique challenges. I know how he feels. I too am blind. Jake was created, in part, out of my own personal experiences. I have faced many of the challenges that Jake faced, and more. In life, we all face challenges. Everyone has something that makes their life harder than the next person's. For me that something is being blind. For you, I don't know what it is but there is something. Sometimes, as we struggle to face life's challenges, we also struggle to hold on to hope or we lose hope all together. For many people, what hope they do have is tied to the things of this world, things that will not last. But, you know what? You can obtain a hope that is eternal. Not just a hope but an assurance. I have that assurance, in Jesus Christ, who is my Lord and Savior. Do you have that assurance? I'm not talking about being a good person or going to church. Is Jesus Christ your Lord and Savior? If He is not or if you really don't know, please read on.

I am going to talk about some scripture here. The full text of the scripture follows or, of course, you can look it up in your own bible, if you have one handy.

How are we saved? Can we be good enough? Romans 3:10 says that no one is righteous and Romans 3:23 says that all have sinned and come short of the glory of God. So no, we cannot be good enough because we all sin.

What do we deserve because of that sin? Read Romans 6:23. The first part says "the wages of sin is death". What are "wages"? They are what we get for doing something, like getting paid for doing a job. So, what we should get for our sin is death. In this case, what

251

does "death" mean? Does it mean God should Kill us? No, of course not. It means eternal spiritual separation from God. After physical death, it also means going to Hell. So, for our sin, we deserve to be eternally separated from God and forever burn in Hell.

So, that's it? No! What does the next part of Romans 6:23 say? It says "but the gift of God is eternal life through Jesus Christ our Lord". How did Jesus pay for this gift of eternal life? 2 Corinthians 5:21 says that Christ never sinned but he took our sins on himself and Romans 5:8 says that He died as punishment for those sins. So, the son of God paid for the most precious gift that we could ever receive with his own blood.

How do we get this gift? Read John 3:16.

For God so loved the world

that he gave his only begotten Son (Jesus)

that whoever believes in him (whoever means everyone)

should not perish, but have everlasting life (not die spiritually and be separated from God)

To get this gift from Jesus, you have to ask him to save you. Romans 10:13 says that "whoever shall call upon the name of the Lord shall be saved".

You have to pray and ask Jesus to save you and that goes something like this: Jesus, I know that I am a sinner and that I deserve to be separated from God for eternity. I know that I don't deserve forgiveness but you died to save me from my sins. I want you to come into my heart and save me and I give my life to you.

When we are saved, we have to repent, which means to turn from our sins (Acts 3:19). Even Christians still sin but we have to try hard not to and always try to do better.

252

We should be baptized after we are saved (Matthew 28:19). Baptism symbolizes his death, burial, and resurrection. This tells the world what we have done.

Did you pray the prayer above or something similar? If you did and you were sincere then your name is now written in the Lam's Book of Life. If you have never prayed that prayer, if you do not have a personal relationship with Jesus Christ, then I urge you to give this your full attention. Nothing is more important. In John 14:6, Jesus said "I am the way, the truth, and the life: no one comes to the Father except through me". Do you know him?

Scripture:

The following scripture is from the New King James Bible, Copyright Thomas Nelson 1982.

Romans 3:10 - As it is written: "There is none righteous, no, not one;

Romans 3:23 - for all have sinned and fall short of the glory of God,

Romans 6:23 - For the wages of sin is death, but the gift of God is eternal life in Christ Jesus our Lord.

2 Corinthians 5:21 - For He made Him who knew no sin to be sin for us, that we might become the righteousness of God in Him.

Romans 5:8 - But God demonstrates His own love toward us, in that while we were still sinners, Christ died for us.

John 3:16 - For God so loved the world that He gave His only begotten Son, that whoever believes in Him should not perish but have everlasting life.

Romans 10:13 - For "whoever calls on the name of the Lord shall be saved."

Acts 3:19 - Repent therefore and be converted, that your sins may be blotted out, so that times of refreshing may come from the presence of the Lord,

Matthew 28:19 - Go therefore and make disciples of all the nations, baptizing them in the name of the Father and of the Son and of the Holy Spirit,

John 14:6 - Jesus said to him, "I am the way, the truth, and the life. No one comes to the Father except through Me.